VALLEY
OF
GOLD

VALLEY
OF
GOLD

•

KENT CONWELL

AVALON BOOKS
THOMAS BOUREGY AND COMPANY, INC.
401 LAFAYETTE STREET
NEW YORK, NEW YORK 10003

PRINTED IN THE UNITED STATES OF AMERICA
ON ACID-FREE PAPER
BY HADDON CRAFTSMEN, SCRANTON, PENNSYLVANIA

To Susan and Amy, two daughters of whom I am very proud, and who have learned that hard work creates good luck. And to my wife, Gayle, who has tolerated me for over a quarter century.

Chapter One

My grandpa always figured that Andrew Jackson, Old Hickory, was about the best president and finest man he ever met. In fact, he was so taken by Jackson, he gave me the old gentleman's name, Andrew Jackson. Stonecipher was our last name, and those three words strung together always managed a laugh or snicker from somewhere.

Andrew Jackson Stonecipher. Kinda fancy, I reckon, for a common cowpoke, but I didn't really mind. Many a frosty night in front of a roaring fireplace I sat spellbound at Grandpa's knee as he regaled me with tales of Andy's stirring deeds. And the truth is, I felt right proud to bear the same handle as the old statesman.

1

But that's where the similarities ended. Old Hickory was a people's man. I was a loner, inclined not to saddle myself with others' problems. The West was a mighty big place, sprawling from the Mississippi to the Pacific, from the Rio Grande to Canada. A smart jasper looked after himself and never butted into anyone's business, but then I met those women and their younkers, and nothing was ever the same afterward.

Strange how one incident can change the direction of a jasper's life.

But like I said, the name Andrew Jackson Stonecipher usually brought a laugh or two, just as it did that evening before the wheezing John Bull 2-4-0 steam locomotive with its funnel-shaped smokestack jumped the tracks and went sliding through the sand, depositing me and half a dozen other unfortunates out in the middle of the hostile Arizona desert.

We were heading northeast back to Tucson on a small spur line that ran down to the silver mines near the border. The small engine pulled a single car with seven passengers, counting me and the conductor, an old man leaking tobacco from the sides of his lips into his straggly beard. His stomach hung over his belt, a perfect match for the potbellied stove in the middle of the car.

Two of the passengers were women with their

youngsters, the older one with a boy and a girl, all three dressed in fine, store-bought clothes; the other, her dark hair pulled into a knot on the back of her head, had a boy, a bright-eyed blond about six or so. Their dress was homespun, linsey and striped cotton.

I'd always been uncomfortable around folks, so as usual, I'd purposely taken up a spot by myself at the end of the coach. To my dismay, nothing would do but the older woman had to drag me into their conversation. "Yoo-hoo, young man. At the end of the car. Young man."

I glanced over my shoulder, and when I saw she was talking to me, I quickly rose, balancing myself against the rocking of the coach as it clattered over the rails. "Yes, ma'am."

"My name is Dora Barton. These are my children, Marline Ray and John Edward." Her voice was coarse, like the cawing of a crow, and her black, crinkled hair looked like a roll of barbed wire with a tiny straw hat perched right in the middle. She nodded to the woman across the aisle. "And this is Miz Grace Miller, and her boy, Otsie," she added with a sniff.

I could see right off she considered herself and her children to be huckleberries and not persimmons, but I nodded, not anxious to involve myself with them. Dora Barton seemed like one of those ladies who could make a dumb cowpoke like me seem even dumber. "Howdy. My name's Stonecipher, ma'am." I smiled at the second woman, whose face seemed filled with weariness and worry. She returned my smile woodenly.

Dora Barton's children snickered at each other as she gushed, "Oh, Mr. Stonecipher. How nice to meet you. Are you going to Tucson?"

"Yes, ma'am."

"Looking for work? If you are, my husband can help. We own the dry goods store in Tucson. The children and me were down visiting my brother who is an important man with the Carreta Mines. He might help you find a job there if you prefer mining work." She paused to catch her breath, and like a runaway locomotive, started right up again. "Of course, I wouldn't like it. Mining is so dirty. But then, the dry goods business is hard work, too . . . just not as dirty."

I shook my head and managed to wedge in a reply. "No, ma'am. I'm not looking for work, but I am obliged." I said no more. The fact that I was meeting a gent from Oregon Territory for a job was my business only.

She hesitated and looked me over like I was a murderer with a meat-ax. I guess she decided I wouldn't do them any harm, so she added,

"Wouldn't you care to come down here and join in our conversation? Help pass the time to Tucson?"

I glanced at the cowpoke who claimed he was our conductor, but he continued to slouch in his seat, snoring, his Western hat pulled down over his eyes. I started to refuse, but the younger woman smiled sadly through the worry on her face, and I had the distinct feeling she wanted me to come down and rescue her from the older lady.

"Well, I wouldn't want to impose, ma'am."

With the shrill screech of steel against steel, the train rounded a curve, and I placed my hand on the seat for balance.

"Oh, dear me, no, Mr. Stonecipher. You're not imposing. Please, join us. But don't be so formal," she added with a giggle. "What is your given name?"

With a grimace, I replied, "Andrew Jackson, ma'am, but my friends call me Andy."

"Andrew Jackson?" She looked at the younger woman and laughed. "Oh, you were named after Stonewall Jackson, then."

"No, ma'am." I groaned inwardly. "Stonewall, he was in the War of Secession, what some call the Civil War. I was named after Old Hickory. He was a general back during the War of 1812." My explanation didn't seem to register, so I prompted her. "The Battle of New Orleans? Louisiana?"

"Oh, you mean that foreign country. I see."

Before I could correct her, she shrugged. "Still, I would find it so emb—"

I don't know what else she was going to say, for just then, the wheels beneath the coach shrieked, and the car lurched, knocking me off my feet.

The next thing I knew, luggage and bodies were flying through the air. My first thought was of that steel potbellied stove ricocheting off the walls of the coach, smashing everything in its way, but I couldn't do anything about it because I was flipping head over heels myself.

The train had jumped the tracks and slammed to its side. Glass shattered, and sand spewed inside like water gushing out of a pump into a horse trough. The coach seemed to slide for hours, but the entire incident lasted no more than a few seconds.

Suddenly, it was over.

I lay motionless, trying to decide if I had been killed or not. When I heard other groans, I figured I was still alive.

Stepping carefully over the sprawled bodies, I checked on the others. They were bruised, and scared, but no one was badly hurt. Mrs. Barton and her offspring were crying. "Help me get the ladies out," I said to the conductor.

Minutes later, we had everyone from the coach.

We checked on the engineer. He was dead, so we buried him.

Dora Barton continued squalling and hugging her children to her. "What are we going to do? What are we going to do?"

"When does another train come through?" I asked the conductor.

He squirted a stream of tobacco juice on the sand at his feet and gestured to the overturned locomotive. Escaping steam hissed and rose into the still air. "It don't. This was the only one."

Mrs. Barton moaned and sagged to the ground, dragging her children with her.

Grace Miller hurried to help the distraught woman.

I studied the old man before me. He squirmed under my gaze, and I knew right then he wasn't going to be any help. "That's the truth," he said, whining. "The Carreta Mines has got only one engine." He gestured to the overturned locomotive. "And that's it."

"But, surely," said the younger woman, "they will send out someone to look for us when we don't show up."

He shrugged. "Be a spell. Tucson ain't expecting us for about a week or so. That's the regular trip. This one was special."

More times than I can count, I've found myself

out on my own with no one to turn to for help, not that I needed anyone. So, as far as I was concerned, this would have been no problem if I'd been by myself, but I wasn't. I had two women, three children, and an old man to worry about.

Grace continued to console Mrs. Barton and her children while at the same time keeping an eye and ear on the conversation between me and the conductor.

The sun was dropping behind the Baboquivari Mountains to the west. "First things first, I reckon. Dark's coming mighty fast. The best place for us tonight is in the coach." I looked back at the conductor. "I don't suppose there's any grub about?"

He shrugged and squirted another stream of tobacco onto the sand. "Not unless them ladies got any."

Grace nodded. "Otsie and me've got some crackers and a tin of sardines we'll share."

Dora Barton had calmed down enough to shake her head emphatically. "We don't have anything. Nothing at all." Her children quickly agreed.

At least we had water. A jasper can get by quite a spell without food, but water, well, now, that's another story. I glanced back to the Baboquivari Mountains. There was food and water among those hills. And that's where we were going the next day.

But I figured morning would be soon enough to spring that surprise on them.

After settling down in the coach, I straightened the stove and we built a small fire inside. The temperature had dropped rapidly, and the fire felt mighty good.

Grace offered me a portion of her crackers and tin of sardines.

I shook my head. "No. You and Mrs. Barton share it with your youngsters."

"Hey," growled the conductor. "What about me? I'm hungry."

"We can wait. The women and children need it more than me or you." I gave his ample belly an appraising look. "Stick another chaw of Red Man in your mouth."

He glared at me, then grabbed a blanket and curled up with his back to the fire.

After sharing the meager meal, the others turned in.

Mrs. Barton and her children whined and carried on, but Grace and her boy, Otsie, said their prayers and slipped under their blankets.

I couldn't help admiring her boy, and the way she was raising him.

Finally, all grew quiet. I lay awake, looking through the windows at the stars slowly moving in their orbits. From where I bunked, I could spot the

Big Dipper. I must have watched it for two hours before I dozed.

The next thing I knew, a faint sound awakened me. I glanced at the Big Dipper. I'd been asleep about an hour, but something had disturbed me. I lay motionless, only my eyes moving. Rattlesnake? Or Indians?

A faint scratching seemed to come from where the Bartons were bedded down. The moonlight shone through the windows overhead, lighting the interior of the overturned coach in black-and-white relief.

A flicker of movement caught my eyes. I rose on my elbow. As I watched, Mrs. Barton tore off two chunks of bread from a whole loaf. She handed one chunk to the girl, Marline Ray. Just as she passed the second to John Edward, she spotted me watching. She froze momentarily. The expression on her face was buried in shadow, but I had the distinct feeling she was daring me to say a word.

I lay back. What I had just witnessed didn't surprise me. People looked after themselves first, others second. Folks like Grace Miller and her boy were the exception, not the rule. Mrs. Barton and her spate of children were the rule. That's why I preferred my own company, or that of a good horse or just a mongrel hound dog.

Sleep refused to come, so I rose silently and

slipped outside, carrying my Brass Boy Henry, a tag stuck on the rifle because of the brass frame. Without a blanket, I shivered, but the crisp air perked me up, cleared my head. I could think.

I leaned against the cowcatcher on the overturned 2-4-0 locomotive, so called because the steam engine had two turning wheels under the front truck and four driving wheels behind. This engine, I noted, had no trailing wheels.

I stared to the northeast. All I saw were stars perched on the ground, but out there somewhere was Tucson. A motley collection of mud huts, grass-and-stick *jacales*, and dingy saloons with dirty canvas ceilings that dared an hombre to step inside. Skinny mules and rangy steers slept in the dusty street, gaunt hounds chased squawking chickens through wide-open doors, and rattlesnakes coiled in the shade cast by the adobe walls.

Wizened *señoras*, sun-blackened skin dry as old leather, fussed over unleavened bread in outdoor bake-ovens. The aroma from the ovens filled the sizzling air with the pungent smell of burning tortillas mixed with the ripe odor of the dead and decaying animals lying about the dusty streets.

Tucson. Fifty miles distant. Dirty, smelly, and dangerous, but right then, it looked like the Promised Land of Canaan. I could be there in a day and a night, then back the next day with help. Even as

I laid my plans, I knew they wouldn't work. These pilgrims couldn't last two days in the desert without help. Not even the old man. I cursed softly.

To the east, false dawn grayed the sky. I peered back into the darkness enveloping the Baboquivaris. "About six miles," I muttered. "I could make it by noon." I caught myself, suddenly embarrassed. My ears burned. "*We* can make it."

I sighed. All these years, I'd always taken care of myself, looked after myself and no one else. It was a hard habit to break, but now, like it or not, I had no choice. I'd get these folks to the Baboquivaris, settle them down in a cave with a few days' grub, and then I could head out for help.

A faint scratching from the coach caused me to look around. Grace Miller climbed out through the open door. She pulled her shawl tightly around her shoulders against the morning chill and peered about. When she saw me, she nodded.

"You're up early, Mr. Stonecipher."

"Yes, ma'am."

She paused by my side, staring out across the vast desert. Several seconds passed and then she spoke in a tiny, childlike voice. "We're in serious trouble, aren't we?"

"Well, ma'am. It isn't like we were heading for a church social or anything like that."

She laughed softly. "You have a talent for understatement, Mr. Stonecipher."

When I didn't reply, she grew silent, hugging her shawl about her shoulders. She cleared her throat. "I'd like to apologize for Mrs. Barton."

I'm not easily taken aback, but that remark surprised me. She could tell because she looked up into my face and quickly added, "I was awake when she divided the bread with her children. She didn't really mean any harm. She just wanted to take care of her own. That's how mothers are."

By now false dawn had given way to early morning. I stared down at my gnarled and lean fingers gripping the Brass Boy Henry. Idly I flexed my fingers, trying to find the right answer. "Well, ma'am, I . . ."

"Please, Mr. Stonecipher. Call me Grace." She laughed nervously. "I still like to think I'm not quite old enough to be a ma'am."

I grinned at her candor. "Yes, ma'am . . . I mean, Grace. It's just that out here, well . . ." I couldn't find the right words to explain what it took to survive in the West, so I just shrugged and replied, "If that's how mothers are, why did you share your grub with us?"

By now, it was light enough to see the blush color her cheeks. "As I remember, Mr. Stonecipher, neither you nor the conductor touched our food."

"That's not the point, Grace. Mrs. Barton was being selfish. I don't care about the reason. Selfish is selfish, no matter the reason. And by the way, I'm not Mr. Stonecipher. I'm Andy, if you don't mind. We're going to be spending a lot of time together the next few days. I reckon we'd all be more comfortable without the formality of drawn-out handles, don't you?" Suddenly, I realized I had committed myself to something other than looking out for myself. I wasn't sure I really liked the idea.

"Yes." She smiled.

By now, the light was sufficient that I could see the twinkle in her eyes. I was surprised for a second time. When she smiled, she was a right attractive woman. Her husband was a lucky man.

I pushed myself off the cowcatcher and nodded to the coach. "We best wake 'em and get started while it's cool."

"Started?" She frowned. "Where to?"

"Yonder." I nodded to the Baboquivaris. "There you'll be safe as in your mother's arms while I go for help."

Grace studied me a moment, then nodded. "I'll wake Otsie."

"Good." I relaxed. Maybe the next few days would be easier than I thought.

Five minutes later, I would have swapped a barroom brawl for the ruckus Dora Barton and the conductor raised.

Chapter Two

Standing outside the overturned coach, I tried to explain to the conductor and Mrs. Barton just why we had to reach the Baboquivaris, but it was like pouring water down a bottomless hole.

Finally, I grew frustrated. I slapped my battered Stetson against my worn jeans and leaned the Brass Boy against the side of the coach while I scratched my head. Some folks were sure a puzzle, and that reminded me again just why I enjoyed being a loner.

When they finished huffing and puffing, I eyed them coldly. "Look. I'm going to tell you one more time, and then I'm leaving. You do what you want. But I promise you that if you stay out here until someone decides to come searching for us, you're going to be up to your neck in rattlesnakes, Indians, and Comancheros, none of which I'd care to take home to introduce to my ma. I grew up around here. I know the Baboquivaris. There's water and grub, nothing fancy, but you'll live until I get back from Tucson with help.''

"Oh, no," whined Dora Barton.

The conductor snorted and squirted a stream of tobacco on the sand at his feet. "You? You don't look like you could make a mile in this wilderness out here." He made a sweeping gesture with his arm.

I knew what they were looking at, a lanky drink of water held together by leathery skin and worn duds. But then, I knew what I could do. I wasn't worried.

"Well, partner, I reckon that's a call you'll have to make, because I'm going." My ears burned with anger, and my eyes swept the onlooking faces. I was ready to walk out on the entire bunch of ungrateful fools. "Anyone who wants to go is welcome, but I'm leaving now."

For a moment, no one spoke, then Grace Miller said, "I'm going. Otsie and I are going with you."

Dora Barton glared at the younger woman. "You . . . you can't." She turned her accusing eyes on the conductor and added, "You'd go off and leave me and my children here with this . . . this . . . cretin?"

The conductor frowned at the word. He looked at me, and I just shrugged. I'd never heard of anything called a "cretin." Some kind of strange animal, I reckoned.

Dora Barton shivered and hugged her youngsters to her. They buried their heads in their ma's bosom and bawled. Grace looked around at me.

I shrugged. "It's a six-hour walk to the mountains. There's a ravine about halfway where we can get out of the sun."

"What about water?" the conductor complained. "There's only one water jug."

I'd forgotten about the water, and suddenly I saw a lever that might force them to go with me. "What about it? You won't need it here."

Mrs. Barton's face twisted into a frown like thunder. "Why not?"

"Because, Mrs. Barton, by nighttime, you'll be dead."

Her face went slack with shock. Her children squalled louder.

"Andy." Grace stepped forward. "You can't go off and leave them without water. It isn't Christian."

"Who said I was a Christian?" I reckoned I was—maybe not what folks call a Christian, but I'd always believed in God, but right then He was not even on my mind. I shrugged and looped the jug over my shoulder. "You ready to go?"

Grace hesitated. She glanced back at Dora Barton. "Please, Mrs. Barton. Andy knows the country. We've got to trust him."

I crossed my fingers, hoping the contrary woman would shed some of her highfalutin stubbornness. If she didn't, I was still going, but the water was a bluff. I couldn't leave anyone without water.

Clearing my throat, I made one last effort to persuade her. "Mrs. Barton. I won't lie and tell you the trip isn't hard. It is, but in the mountains, I know of a couple of hidden valleys with icy water and cool shade. In one of them is a small cave that you can sleep in at night and be as safe as if you were in your own bed."

"Wait a minute."

We looked around at the conductor. He pointed to my feet. I wore moccasins. "Look at him. For all we know, he's some kind of half-breed Injun. I ain't trusting him. He's probably got Injun friends and squaws."

For a moment, I considered busting him between the eyes with my fist or the butt of my Henry, but then I could see no sense in smashing my knuckles or breaking my rifle on pure ignorance.

I shrugged. "I grew up with the Apache. My grandpa died when I was eight." I nodded back to the east. "About fifty miles that way. Apache found me and took me in. I lived with them until I was fifteen, and then the war came along. So, now you know about me, and you think what you want. I'm heading for the Baboquivaris."

"Not me." The conductor snorted. "I'm staying here."

I glared at him. "That don't bother me one bit, but if the women go, you best find you something to hold a little water, because we're taking the jug."

"There ain't nothing," he said. "I'll die of thirst."

"Get the sardine tin from last night."

He looked at me in disbelief. "The sardine tin. You know how much that'll hold?"

I raised my Brass Boy Henry and laid it in the crook of my arm, at the same time cocking the hammer. "Mister, that tin will hold all I'm going to allow you."

He stared at me with a look that promised murder. Finally, his shoulders sagged. "Okay. I'll go."

Grace squeezed Mrs. Barton's arm. "Please. Think about your children."

Dora Barton tossed her head. "All right, but . . ." She warned me with her eyes. "I will not be hurried."

*   *   *

I can't say I hurried her. I tried, but the first leg, which should have taken three hours, took five. The blistering sun beat down from directly overhead by the time we stumbled into the narrow ravine and took refuge under the dappled shade of some wiry mesquite and paloverde.

The children had long since stopped crying. Marline Ray still pouted and whined, but John Edward seemed taken with the idea of traipsing across the desert. At times, both he and Otsie ranged several yards ahead of us. I wasn't too worried about rattlesnakes, for only fools like us wandered about in the middle of the day; however, I wasn't any too anxious to be out here after dark.

The conductor hadn't said a word. When we stopped for a break, he seated himself away from us. When we set out, he lingered behind.

I didn't care. All I wanted to do was reach the inviting ramparts of the Baboquivaris and settle in around a small campfire with fish or rabbit roasting over the flames.

The afternoon leg began about two o'clock, but just before we got started, I climbed up on the rim of the ravine and spotted something that sent icy shivers through my body. A cloud of dust. Back in the direction of the wreck.

"Let's go," I said, leading them from the ravine. From time to time throughout the afternoon, I threw a fast glance over our backtrail. The dust was still back there, drawing closer. I kept quiet. Maybe it was help, but I doubted it.

To my surprise, we made good time, but not good enough. At dusk, we were still a mile from the foothills. Quickly, I arranged the pilgrims in single file, insisting they follow in my tracks.

"Oh, Mama," whined Marline Ray. "This is so silly."

I fixed her with a piercing stare. "Not as silly as fangs this long going into your leg, Missy." I held my finger and thumb two inches apart.

After that, I didn't have any trouble with them, not even the conductor, who didn't linger too far back on this last leg. I swept three or four fat rattlers out of the way, picking them up with the muzzle of my Brass Boy and flinging them aside. After the first one, I noticed everyone seemed to scrunch up a little more behind me.

The stars were out when we reached the foothills where I decided we would spend the night. After putting together a small fire behind several large boulders, I scrounged up a meal for the seven of us, taking care to keep the source of the white meat to myself.

"This is very good, Mr. Stonecipher," said Dora

Barton, her face grimy and her hair stringy from the day's trek across the desert.

"It sure is," exclaimed John Edward, wolfing down a large chunk of meat.

In fact, they all seemed to be enjoying the repast, none bothering to question where I'd found grub so fast. I didn't volunteer. Some folks can't stomach rattlesnake, and I had the distinct feeling Dora Barton and her offspring were among those.

During the night, I slipped up above the camp and peered back into the desert, searching for a distant fire. Nothing. That convinced me. Whoever was out there was staying hidden. That signified no good news.

A fresh breeze brushed across my face, clean and sweet-tasting, and for the moment, making me forget the obligations I had taken on. Being a lone wolf was a good life. I could go where I wanted, stay as long as I cared, and pull out when the mood hit.

After the war, I had traveled the country, seeing what was out there. From the rolling breakers on the North Carolina coast to the stark, black rocky bluffs rising from the roaring sea in Oregon Territory, I'd savored the beauty and freedom of this magnificent country. I was perfectly content as I was. What else was there?

Behind me, on the towering peaks of the Baboquivaris, an owl hooted. Moments later, a rabbit squealed. I grinned inwardly, wryly. Even owls have obligations. But the difference between me and the owl was that as soon as I got these pilgrims back to Tucson, I was shed of them. Free again. The poor owl would never be free. He and his mate had a clutch of owlets, and when the little ones flew the nest, another clutch came along. No end to it.

I shook my head. "Stop daydreaming," I whispered to myself. "You got enough on your mind now." I glanced back down the slope to our camp. Next morning, we needed to pull out early. Build up the fire and leave it behind. Silently, I crept back to camp.

A movement in the shadows of a boulder froze me. I whipped my knife from its sheath, and then Grace Miller stepped into the moonlight.

"Is something wrong, Andy?" Her voice was edged with concern. "I saw you leave."

For a moment, I considered lying to her, but she appeared to have a backbone of iron-hard mesquite, while the others were more like dry willow branches that broke at the slightest pressure. "We've been followed."

Instinctively, she pressed her fist against her lips and peered over her shoulder into the night. "Who?"

I slid my knife back into its sheath. "Pimo. Papago. Comancheros. Owlhoots. Who knows? But they're out there following our tracks. I spotted their dust back at the wreck after we left the ravine."

"What are we going to do?"

"Keep going." I hooked my thumb over my shoulder. "Once we get situated up there, we'll be fine. We'll pull out early." I paused, then added deliberately, "But I don't want the others to know about this. We can't afford any delays. If they learn someone's behind us, they'll want to wait around just in case it's help from the mines."

"And ... you don't think it is?" There was a note of hope in Grace's voice.

"No. Too soon. Like the conductor said, Tucson wasn't even expecting us. The Carreta Mines don't look for the train back for a week." I looked over her head into the pool of blackness covering the desert. "No. Whoever's out there ... they're not our friends."

As I expected, there was the typical grousing from the Bartons and the conductor when we moved out later that morning, but they did as I asked. I said nothing about the men following. I didn't want any more distractions than we already had.

We had just entered a patch of juniper and cedar on the mountain slope when the conductor yelled, "Take a look. Down there. A horse! A horse!"

Down below, grazing on some patches of bunchgrass in a small basin, was a broomtailed sorrel so thin that you could see every bone in her body. It didn't take a second look to know that feeble old nag was all tuckered out, turned loose by some cruel owner to die on its own.

Dora Barton exclaimed, "A horse! Get it, Mr. Stonecipher. Hurry. He's our salvation. Hurry!"

Before I could reply, the conductor let out a yelp and rushed down the slope toward the sorrel, sliding and stumbling over the rocks and shrubs. I frowned, trying to guess what he had in mind. The animal needed weeks of good graze before she would amount to anything more than bones and skin. Within the week, we would be back in Tucson.

I shook my head. The conductor's behavior made no sense. Or it didn't until he reached the animal, and then I understood. Moving quickly for a fat man, he rigged a hackamore from his belt, led the nag to a boulder, and climbed on the frail animal's back. The poor creature sagged.

In the next moment, he wheeled around and spurred the animal back into the desert, heading in the direction of Tucson, arms and legs flapping.

Dora Barton gasped. "Look! Look! He's leaving us." She rushed over to me and started pounding my shoulder. "Mr. Stonecipher, Mr. Stonecipher. Stop him! He's leaving us. He's running away. Shoot him!"

Marline Ray and John Edward ran shouting after the conductor, both stumbling over the loose rocks and tumbling headlong down the slope, ending up in a pile of bleeding elbows and squalling tears.

Grace Miller looked on silently, holding her son's hand, her face hard, her eyes filled with a mixture of hurt and anger.

A cloud of dust billowed up from behind the galloping horse. We continued to watch helplessly until the conductor disappeared into the distance behind the puffs of dust kicked up by the sorrel.

Far out in the desert, another ribbon of dust billowed into the clear blue sky, angling away from the Baboquivaris, heading to intercept the conductor.

Grace saw the dust also. "Look—out there."

Dora Barton stopped pounding on my shoulder and stared into the desert. "Look . . . look. Help is here." She started shouting and waving her arms. "Help! Help!"

I had been cursing the conductor, but now I felt sorry for the jasper. He had brought it on himself though. By trying to save his hide at our expense, he hurried his own death. I shook my head. No, I couldn't curse the man any longer. Besides, I told myself as I glanced back at the converging ribbons of dust, I didn't even know the hombre's name.

Suddenly, I felt Dora Barton pounding on my shoulder again. "Stop them. Call them over here."

Gently, I seized her wrists. "Be quiet, Mrs. Barton. Those riders won't help. They're out to kill us."

Chapter Three

We gathered the Barton children and hid among the cedars and junipers until both trails of dust disappeared beyond the horizon.

I turned to the ladies and children and explained our situation. Their faces reflected their fear. "We're going to be just fine. Do what I say, and I promise you, we'll be okay."

The Barton children buried their faces in their mother's arms and cried, but Otsie stared up at me solemnly.

"You hear? Everyone hear? Don't argue, just do what I say."

Grace and Otsie nodded. Dora Barton and her offspring just stared at me.

I led them high into the Baboquivaris, and mid-afternoon, we paused outside a passage hidden behind a thick growth of creosote and buckbrush. Once again, Dora Barton balked like a mule, refusing to enter the cave, but when Grace and Otsie followed me in, the older woman tagged along.

A few minutes later, we entered a small valley my Apache father, Horse of Water, had shown me. The valley was sacred, and I'd never returned after he and the others in his *ranchería* were massacred.

I didn't figure he would mind, for I didn't plan on revealing its secret, just taking advantage of its cover and protection for a few days. I considered making smoke, informing White Eye, my brother, we were here, but decided against it. Other eyes might spot the smoke.

The valley was the dream of every man, forty acres of lush pasture dotted with majestic loblollies, a cold, bottomless lake in the very center, and a snug cave in the wall of one of the vertical cliffs that almost completely enclosed the valley, shutting it off from the rest of the world except through a hidden entrance.

"Why, it's beautiful!" Grace exclaimed as we exited the mountain onto a broad ledge some hundred feet above the valley floor.

Dora Barton sniffed. "Where's the water?"

"Down there." I led the way through the pines

to the base of the trail. "You go on to the lake. Wash up. John Edward, you fill the water jug. I'll rustle us up some grub and build a fire in the cave."

They glanced around. "What cave?" Otsie asked.

"Up there. About a third of the way up the cliff. Everyone see it?"

As one, they nodded.

"The trail up to it is about a hundred feet to the left. It leads along the side of the bluff." I squinted my eyes and nodded upon spotting the log. "Just before you reach the cave, the trail will end, but there is a log that will take you across to the other trail. Once you freshen up, I'll meet you up there, at the log."

Dora Barton gasped. "You're not going to leave us alone here, are you? What about those riders?"

Marline Ray whined, "What about wild animals? Bears?"

I chuckled. "Not in here, child. You'll be safe. No one knows of this valley except me." I started to add that the Apache knew of it, but I couldn't see any sense in worrying them over nothing. If the Apache did show up, they would remember me. I still bore the scar for which I earned my Apache name, Bear Claw.

In a small cove on the opposite side of the lake, I quickly speared a dozen trout, then retreated to the cave where I built a small fire and put the fish on spits.

Once the fish were baking, I headed back down the trail to the log, a thick pine that bridged the thirty-foot break in the trail. The log was solid, no more than a year old. An unbidden grin came to my lips, and I stared overhead at the sheer bluffs reaching to the brittle blue sky.

The Apache never forgot.

Soon, I heard the women and children coming.

Otsie and Grace came first. Like a mountain goat, Otsie pranced across the log. Grace, using her left hand to steady herself against the granite walls, tiptoed after her son. I couldn't help noticing she moved almost like an Indian, light as a feather, almost floating.

Dora Barton recoiled at the sight of the log and plopped herself down on the trail. "Not me. I will not cross that log." She gestured to the slope of talus a hundred feet below. "Look how far to the ground."

I rolled my eyes and turned my attention to the children. "All right, Marline Ray. You come across first."

She shook her head and backed away.

"You show her how, John Edward," I said, hoping to shame the girl and her mother.

Reluctantly, the twelve-year-old boy stepped forward. He was scared. I could see it in his eyes, the way they darted from his mother to me and then to Otsie. "The log is steady, boy. Just step on it and walk across."

"Don't you dare, John Edward," snapped his mother.

He licked his lips and looked at me hopefully. "It . . . it won't fall?"

Nearing exasperation, I said, "Watch." I walked out on the log and jumped up and down. It didn't move. I jammed my fists in my hips. "Now are you coming? Or do you want Otsie to hold your hand?"

My last words got to him. His face darkened, and he glared at me. "Nobody is going to hold my hand."

"John Edward!" shouted his mother. "Did you hear me? Don't you dare. That log is too danger—"

He jumped up on the log and hurried across, cutting off his mother's order in mid-sentence. He stepped to the ground and glared up at me, his eyes squinting, his jaw jutting. "See? I can do it myself. I don't need no help."

I shook my head. "By jasper, you did it, boy. Reckon I was wrong. Now let's get your sister and mother over."

After much coaxing, Marline Ray eased over, but her mother refused to budge.

By now, I was growing angry. I despised mule-headed stubbornness, and that straggly haired lady plopped on her bustle across the log had me at the end of my rope.

"Mrs. Barton. If you don't come over right now, I'm coming across, throwing you over my shoulder like a side of beef, and hauling your carcass back over here. Now, you'll probably fight me, which means we'll both fall off that log and kill ourselves dead, but ma'am, you're coming over here, or we're going down there." I nodded to the talus below.

I handed Otsie my Brass Boy and in half a dozen steps, I reached the other side.

Her eyes bugged out. She struggled to reach her feet before I got to her, but she was too slow. She started squealing. "Don't you dare. My husband will have you arrested. John Edward! Stop him! Stop him!"

I grabbed one arm, dropped into a squat, and yanked her into my shoulder. I stood quickly, and my knees almost buckled. I groaned. That bulky dress she wore sure hid a lot of beef. She must've been packing twenty or thirty pounds more than I expected.

"Stop squirming," I growled, eyeing the log warily. Someone lighter, I could have danced across, but with her— Well, I tried not to think about it.

By now she was squealing and squirming like a

stolen pig, but I was determined. The one advantage I had was that the log was against the side of the cliff. I could brace my shoulder against the granite wall.

"Here we go," I said, steadying my wobbly knees and catching a deep breath.

She squirmed and squealed even louder.

I bellowed out, "Mrs. Barton!"

For a moment, she fell silent.

In a cold, menacing voice strained with anger, I said, "If you say one more word or squirm one more time, as soon as I get you to the other side, I'm going to put you over my knee and spank the daylights out of you."

She froze.

I didn't hesitate. I had a deadweight on my shoulder, but at least it wasn't squirming like a nest of snakes. Quickly, I stepped on the log, and feeling the rough bark through my leather moccasins, eased across without a hitch and gently stood her on the trail.

"Now," I said, staring down at her, "that wasn't bad, was it?"

She shot me a look that vowed she'd cut my throat at the first opportunity. "Humph!" She spun on her heel and stormed into the cave.

I glanced at Grace, who gave me a sheepish grin.

All I could do was shrug. At least we were safe for the night.

After a filling supper of broiled trout, everyone settled back and relaxed, enjoying the leaping flames of the small fire.

Grace Miller broke the silence. "You've been here before, Andy."

It wasn't a question, but an observation. "Yep. Years back."

Mrs. Barton and her youngsters stared at me curiously. John Edward leaned forward. "When you lived with the Apache?"

"John Edward," Mrs. Barton snapped. "Hush!"

I grinned at the boy. "Yes." Gesturing to the rear of the cave, I continued. "The cave twists and turns back into the mountain. I've been told it comes out back deep somewhere, but I've never tried it. The few times I came here, I was with my Apache father, Horse of Water, and my brother, White Eye." I chuckled at the memory. "He kept a tight rein on us. He never let us go back there."

Otsie peered over his shoulder and scooted closer to his mother. Grace smiled.

"But what if the Apache come while we're here?" asked Marline Ray.

Mrs. Barton's eyes popped open wide. She gasped. "Heavens! I didn't think about that." She turned accusing eyes on me. "You've led us in here to be slaughtered. We'll all die.'' She struggled to her feet. ''Come, children. Hurry. Hurry! We've got to leave this place before the savages get us.''

I stared at her in disbelief.

Grace rose quickly. ''Mrs. Barton. Please, be calm. There's no danger here.''

Her eyes wild with fear, Dora Barton shrugged off Grace's hand. ''We'll all die.'' Tears flooded down her pasty cheeks. ''We'll all die out here in this godforsaken wilderness, and no one will ever find us.'' She hugged her children to her side. ''Oh, my poor children. My poor, poor children.''

Marline Ray was hugging her mother and crying by now, but John Edward, his face jammed into his mother's side by her arm, looked at me quizzically, puzzled by the sudden outburst.

I remained squatted by the fire, figuring the frightened woman might go berserk if I came near. ''Mrs. Barton.''

She ignored me.

''Mrs. Barton.'' I spoke louder.

She broke off her wailing in the middle of a screech and stared at me, wide-eyed, like I was a blood-covered killer with a knife between my teeth. ''Don't come near me. I'll scream.''

Leaning back against the wall of the cave, I replied, ''You're doing a fair job of screaming now, and I promise you, if there are any Indians out there, you've let them know we're here.''

Her eyes glared at me, then cut to the mouth of the cave. When she looked back at me, her bushy eyebrows furrowed into a frown, I nodded.

In a soft, gentle voice, I said, ''Just calm down. No one is going to bother you in here. Besides, if you leave, you've got the log to cross, and if you cross it, then you're out in the middle of the darkness with nowhere to go.''

She seemed to calm somewhat, but she still had John Edward's face scrunched into her side, and he was squirming like a little snake trying to free himself.

''Now, I want you to listen. All of you.'' I looked at Grace. ''You're safe in here. You got wood for the fire; there's water. Nothing to worry about.'' Slowly, I rose. ''I'm going out. I won't be long. I just want to find out about those riders we saw today.''

I reached for my Brass Boy. ''Mrs. Barton, can you use a rifle?''

She stiffened up like a plank. She gasped and turned loose of John Edward's head when she pressed her hand to her heart. ''Heavens, no. A rifle? No! No.''

''I can.'' Grace stepped forward. ''I know how

to use one. Before Otsie's father, my husban—''
She paused, then said, "I know how to use one."

"Good." I handed it to her. "It's a Henry. Forty-four rimfire. Lever action. Fifteen cartridges in the magazine. That's all I've got, but it'll be enough."

She stared up at me soberly, her eyes questioning.

"I don't expect any trouble for you. Like I said, only the Apache know of this valley. If one comes before I get back, tell him Bear Claw, son of Horse of Water, brought you here. Can you remember that?"

"Yes." She nodded.

By now, Mrs. Barton had stopped shaking. She appeared to have herself under control.

I continued. "All I want to do is find out if the riders came back. Tomorrow, I'll gather you enough grub to last a week, and then I'll take out for Tucson. It'll take me about a day and night to get there, another day and night back. That means that in three days, help will be here. In four days, you'll all be safe in Tucson."

No one replied. They just stared at me. Finally, Marline Ray spoke up, her voice thin and frail. "I don't want you to go out tonight."

Taken aback by her request, I stared at her in surprise. "I've got to."

"But . . . but, what if something happens to you? What about us? What will we do?"

That was the one question I had hoped no one would ask, for there was only one answer, and that answer didn't offer enough hope to hang your hat on, not for these pilgrims.

She repeated the question, her young face pale with fear. "What are we going to do if something happens to you?"

I looked at each of them. In Grace and Otsie's faces, I saw determination, strength, but in the others, only weakness. I cleared my throat. "If something happens to me, then you've got to get to Tucson yourself. You leave this valley, and head northeast across the desert. Travel only when it's cool. When you build a fire, make it small, and keep it hidden."

I paused and cursed to myself. What was I trying to do—in two minutes give them survival knowledge that it took me twenty-seven years to learn? If something happened to me, they didn't have any more chance than a dry leaf in the middle of a prairie fire.

"Look. Nothing's going to happen to me. I'll be back in a few hours." I nodded to the Brass Boy. "Just don't get reckless with that thing when I come back, you hear?"

Grace smiled. "I hear."

"Now listen. Just so you'll know who's coming and going. When I come back, I'll give three short whistles, like this.'' I demonstrated an undulating call—*keree, keree, keree.* "It's the song of the rock wren.''

Otsie grinned. "I can do that.'' Without waiting, he mimicked my call.

I shrugged and arched an eyebrow. His call was better than mine.

"Just don't forget, hear?''

"Don't worry.''

Chapter Four

The night air was crisp, and the moon lit the valley with a cool, bluish glow. Travel was easy down the mountain trail and across the rocky slopes to the passage leading outside.

Inside the passage, I had to feel my way along, opting against building a torch. No one knew of this cave. No one except Apaches. While I figured it unlikely, there was always a chance that one of the tribe had gone bad and had fallen in with the wrong kind. One could even be outside right now, so there was no sense in drawing any attention.

Fifteen minutes later, I paused just inside the mouth of the passage, peering through the buck-brush and creosote shrubs that hid the entrance. The ghostly blue talus slopes of the Baboquivaris and the desert beyond were silent and empty, with no sign of man or fire.

I considered remaining in the passage, none too anxious to make the acquaintance of any rattlesnake enjoying the warmth of the rocky slopes. On the other hand, from where I stood, I had a limited view.

Carefully, I eased through the shrubs and crossed the talus to the shadows of a clutch of junipers. Suddenly, I froze as a faint tendril of wood smoke drifted past on the currents sweeping up the side of the mountain. I stared down into the darkness.

Nothing.

I sniffed. There it was again. Wood smoke.

On a distant slope to the north, a rabbit squealed.

Down below, a horse whinnied.

Up above, a rock clattered.

Instinctively, my hand went to my knife, and I froze, listening, not moving from the shadows. As far as I knew, someone might be behind me, farther up the slope. My heart thudded in my chest. All I could do now was wait and curse myself for the mess I was in.

If I'd stayed down in the Sierra Madres, none of this would have happened. If I hadn't decided to go to Tucson, then I wouldn't have lost my horse and been forced to take the train. If . . . If—the story of my life.

A rattle of shifting rocks from above jerked me back to my present predicament. I pressed deeper into the shadows of the juniper. My fingers tightened about the handle of my knife.

The clatter of dislodged rocks continued, punctuated by an occasional mutter and the clink of rowels against rocks. Moments later, a dark figure passed several yards to my right, stumbling for his balance as he made his way down the slope of talus. He was tall and lanky. His wide-brimmed hat had a Montana crown, and he wore two six-guns, strapped low.

After he passed below a patch of juniper lower on the slope, I rose to a crouch and quickly followed, hoping any noise I made would be lost in the commotion he was stirring up. Just to be on the safe side, I palmed my Colt.

In the next instant, I almost jumped out of my skin, for a dark, sinuous shape slithered across my path not five feet in front of me. Instantly, I brought the muzzle of my six-gun to bear on the rattler, but he must have been as frightened as me, for he skittered across the talus and disappeared into the shadows of another juniper.

I remained motionless for several seconds, waiting for my heart to creep back down out of my throat. I had never been scared of snakes, but when one pops up on me out of nowhere, well, that's different.

The jasper below continued his noisy way down the slope.

I followed, watching my feet. Ten minutes later, I dropped into a crouch behind a thick loblolly. Below in a shallow ravine flickered a small fire. As best I could tell, five figures hunched around it, four of them leaning against the side of the arroyo. The newcomer made six, unless there was a guard out.

They weren't just passing by. Why would one have been up on the slope? No, they were after something—probably us. I crept forward, silent as a bobcat, wary as a mountain lion, keeping one eye on the fire, one for the guard, and a third for rattlers. Finally, I dropped to my belly and wiggled forward until I settled in behind a patch of sage several yards above and downwind from the camp, where I could only catch bits and pieces of their conversation.

The dissonant smell of acrid creosote and rich coffee wafted up to me.

To my horror, my stomach growled. I rolled my eyes, unable to believe what I had just heard. That was all I needed, sneaking up on a band of owlhoots and then being given away by a traitorous stomach. But they didn't seem to hear. I eased forward.

"Nothing," growled the cowpoke wearing the Montana crown. "Didn't see nothing."

A figure leaning against a boulder in the middle of the ravine spoke. His voice was like gravel. "They didn't sprout no wings and fly away. He said some hombre brought women and children up here. Ain't no way I'm going to turn loose of that kind of money."

Comancheros! I clenched my teeth. Comancheros. Border scum who stole women and children to sell across the border. I flexed my fingers on the butt of my Colt.

"They mighta done took off, Tulsa Jack. They had all day," said a third voice from one of the figures leaning against the side of the ravine.

Tulsa Jack snorted. "Idiot. Where would they go? We would've spotted them. Naw, they're up there somewhere, and come morning, we're gonna find 'em."

"What if we don't?"

"We'll keep looking. When we find 'em, we'll have us some fun first."

Several chuckles around the fire sent cold chills through my veins. I just thought we had trouble before. Right now, I would have settled for the middle of a stampede. I studied our situation.

I could jump up and start blasting away with my six-gun, but then what would happen when I ran out of shells? Those hombres weren't going to wait around for me to reload. Or I could spook their horses. Or I could take care of them one at a time over the next few days.

No. The smartest move on my part was to return to the valley and wait 'em out. But I didn't like that idea because waiting meant I'd placed the initiative on someone else, that I would be sitting back and waiting for them to make the first move.

That was not the aggressive behavior of an Apache, but I had the women and children to consider.

Moments later, my decision was made for me.

Just before I scooted away, a shadow glided into the firelight. I couldn't make him out, but he was Indian. That was certain.

Tulsa Jack grunted. "Well? Snag here didn't find nothing."

"I find nothing. But it is late. When the sun rises, I will find them. From the stories of the old men, there are two, maybe three canyons, all hidden. The whites must be in one of them."

"You better find them, Injun, or I'll skin you alive," Tulsa Jack growled. "You worthless . . ." The large man shoved the Indian aside and squatted with his back to the boulder.

Another round of chuckles broke the cool night air.

The Indian sat apart from the white men.

Moving carefully, I backed away. Now I couldn't wait. If the Indian looked long enough, he'd spot the hidden entrance to the passage. I wondered at his tribe. Pimo? Papago?

No matter. I had to move fast. Maybe I could get rid of a couple before they knew I was coming after them. Then, instead of seven to one, I would only have five to worry about.

Shucking my shirt, I buttoned it up and tied off my neck and sleeves, making a secure bag. I cut several strips from one of the sleeves to make a six-foot-long tie for the neck of the bag. Next, I cut a six-foot branch with a fork at one end, each tine of the fork about six inches.

Then I went rattlesnake hunting.

The rocky slopes were cooling from the chill air, driving the rattlers back to their dens. Their dark, sinuous shapes were easy to spot and easier to catch. I jabbed the fork over their bodies just behind the head, then grasping the head, dropped the serpent into the shirt bag. I quickly tied off the neck, and went after another rattler.

Within twenty minutes, I had four angry rattlers. I wanted more, but the branch was not stiff enough to support more. Besides, I kept wondering if the buttons on my shirt would hold. Their tough, muscular bodies stretched the well-worn fabric of the shirt.

Action would get pretty exciting if the buttons popped off while I was holding the bag and those irate rattlers came boiling out. *No,* I told myself. *Be satisfied with what you have. These four'll make it interesting enough around the fire.*

Creeping back to the ravine, I placed the neck of the bag in the fork. I tied the strips of shirtsleeve about the neck and twisted them around the branch so that I could shove the bag ahead of me to the edge of the ravine. A sharp yank on the strips would loosen the knot holding the neck.

The plan worked perfectly, except the rattlesnakes doubled back, directly toward me. When you only find six feet separating you from four wrathful rattlers, you don't waste time thinking. I yanked on the branch, which jerked my shirt in the air behind the snakes.

In one swift motion, they spun and hurled themselves at the shirt waving in the breeze. I felt a jerk and heard the shirt tear. Their momentum carried them over the edge of the ravine onto the men squatting around the fire.

In the next instant, screams erupted from below and the night was shattered by gunfire and shouts. I didn't wait around. Clutching the branch, I hightailed it through the night back up the slope, pausing when I reached the loblollies above the camp.

The camp was in turmoil.

Cowpokes jumped and danced about, shooting at the ground. Slugs ripped the campfire apart. Horses whinnied, frightened by the commotion.

Tulsa Jack's raspy voice overpowered the commotion. ''The horses! Get the horses. They're stampeding.''

I chuckled as I untied my shirt and started to slip it on, but it was soaked with venom. I had a few scratches on my back, so I didn't take a chance. I'd wash it out back at the lake. In the meantime, I settled down to watch the fun below.

But there was no show. The campfire went out. All I could do was listen as voices chased the horses through the foothills and into the desert. From time to time out in the desert, a scream and a gunshot echoed through the night as a cowpoke stumbled across another rattlesnake. From the number of screams and gunshots, the rattlers must've been having some kind of convention out there.

I couldn't help laughing to myself. Maybe the owlhoots would give up. For several minutes, I crouched, staring down upon the camp. Nothing moved.

Satisfied, I headed back to the valley. Then I hesitated. Maybe I should hang around just in case a stray horse came by. That would cut my journey to Tucson in half.

So, I found a snug retreat in a patch of juniper, and after making sure I didn't have any companions with rattles on their tails, I settled down to wait and watch.

Slowly, the commotion died away. An hour later, a small fire punched a hole in the darkness about a mile out in the desert. From time to time, figures moved in front of it.

I glanced back into the ravine. Darkness filled the arroyo like black water. If anyone was down there, I'd have to wait until sunup to see them.

Chapter Five

The breeze drifting up the mountain slope from the desert brought the sharp aroma of sage and creosote. From time to time when the tart odor became too strong, I crushed juniper needles and inhaled their pine-fresh fragrance.

Soon, I grew drowsy. All movement had ceased around the fire, so I eased back to the valley where I washed my ripped shirt and hung it up to dry. I lay on a thick bed of grass and quickly fell asleep.

With the sun, I arose, slipped into my damp shirt, and caught some more fish for breakfast and wasted no time heading back to the cave. I had a great deal of work to do before I could push off for Tucson.

For the most part, everyone was in a fair mood

51

except for Mrs. Barton and her daughter, Marline Ray, but after they filled up on fresh trout, even their mood improved.

Grace picked a flake of white flesh from a bone. "Did you see anyone out there, Andy?"

"No. Everything seems okay," I replied. The lie didn't bother me. They didn't need to know the truth, at least not right now. Later on, before I left, but not now. I wanted them nice and calm while I gathered grub to get them over the next few days.

I licked my fingers and stood up. "Okay, boys. I'm going to show you how to catch fish. The next couple of days, you'll have to shoulder the load of bringing in food."

Otsie's eyes grew wide, but not as wide as the grin that leaped to his face.

John Edward glanced sidelong at his ma, who looked up at me in shock. "Fish? In the water?"

I just stared at her, thinking I'd missed something. Finally, I nodded. "Yes. That's . . . where they are, in the water."

She grabbed her son's arm. "Not John Edward. He's too young. He might drown."

Grace glanced at her, then looked up at me.

"No," I replied. "The water is about knee-deep where they'll be. They're not going to drown."

John Edward pulled away from his mother.

"Please, Ma. Let me fish. I'll be okay. I won't drown."

Marline Ray twisted her face in a sneer. "You will too, you silly boy. You'll get out there and drown yourself dead."

He spun on her. "You shut up, or I'll whop you upside the head."

Mrs. Barton joined in. "Children. Children. Stop the fighting."

Marline Ray stuck her tongue out at John Edward. "Yaa, yaa, yaa. Drown, drown, drown."

That's when he popped her, right on the nose.

The girl froze, stared wide-eyed in disbelief, then burst into a storm of squalls.

Mrs. Barton lurched for John Edward, snagged his arm, and with surprising strength, jerked him over her lap and began walloping his behind.

He screamed.

Marline Ray screamed.

I just shook my head and backed away, grateful that I would soon be away from the madhouse. As I started across the log, I felt something touch my hand. It was Otsie.

"Can I still fish, Mr. Stonecipher?"

I glanced back at the cave. Grace stood on the ledge in front of the mouth. She nodded. "Sure," I said. "Come on, boy."

Before I knew what was happening, he stuck his

tiny hand in mine. I looked down, surprised. He grinned up at me. I chuckled. "Let's go."

Inside the cave, the bellowing continued. Now, I've heard sow pigs squeal when their little ones are taken, and I've listened to the bawling of mama cows trying to get to their calves, but never had I heard a commotion like that going on up in the cave.

Suddenly, a thought hit me. I looked around the valley at the granite walls rising to the clouds. The walls kept the sound from spilling into the desert, but what if someone had climbed up above?

Muttering a curse at my own dull wit, I turned back to the cave.

The screaming stopped. Moments later, John Edward ran out. He stopped and looked back. "I'm going." He bolted across the log and skidded to a halt in front of me. "I'm ready."

I looked down at him, then back at the cave, expecting to see his ma come boiling out like a two-ton longhorn frothing at the mouth.

Grace glanced back in the cave, then shrugged at me.

"Let's go, then."

Both youngsters caught on fast. I showed John Edward how to build a holding pond by weaving grass and flexible branches into a net, and then I put Otsie to setting snares along rabbit trails. I started to warn them about a small passage through which the narrow stream emerged from the canyon walls.

The fissure was difficult to ford. At the rear of the fissure, there was a small hollow where the ground was littered with gold nuggets, for years a source of instant money for the Apache.

Finally, I decided not to mention the passage. I remembered enough about my own childhood to know that the surest way to get a boy to do something is to forbid him to do it. So I kept quiet. A thicket of briars jammed the entrance. I felt certain the secret of the Apache would remain safe.

While they worked, I sneaked back through the hidden passage and peered out over the desert. No one was in sight. I frowned, puzzled. Had the Comancheros given up? I didn't think so. Did my snakes cut down the odds? I had no way of knowing.

Shaking my head, I started to turn back, but the clatter of a rock tumbling down the slope caught my attention. The next thing I knew, several rocks flashed past the hidden opening and tumbled on down the slope.

Someone was up above. I pressed back into the darkness, holding my breath. I heard a grunt, and then more rocks fell. A shadow fell across the opening, hesitated, then disappeared.

I moved to the entrance and knelt behind the creosote and buckbrush. The figure, an Indian dressed in white man's clothes down to brogans, came into my view on my left. I watched until he disappeared behind a patch of juniper. Moments later, he emerged and continued down the mountainside. I guessed he was Papago or Pima. I guessed the first, for many of the tribe had adopted the ways of the white man, and a cigarette dangled from his lips.

I followed, hiding among the junipers and loblollies.

At the bottom of the slope, the Papago disappeared into another patch of juniper. Moments later, he reappeared with five white men. They spoke and gestured in my direction. The Papago pointed at the rimrock far above my head.

Five white men and the Indian. Six. Last night, there were seven. A shiver ran through my bones. Looked like I'd managed to rid myself of one hombre, thanks to the rattlesnakes.

I glanced over my shoulder toward the hidden passage. Should I return? Go on with my plan? Or wait?

The six owlhoots decided for me. With the Papago leading the way, the gang began climbing the slope, heading directly for me.

Muttering a curse, I looked around frantically. My only hope was that the dense growth of junipers and loblollies would hide me while I slipped away. Dropping to my stomach, I snaked across the pine needles and rocks to a small hogback ridge. Like a rattler, I slithered over the crest and pressed down behind the sawtooth granite protruding into the air.

Sweat poured off my face, dripping to the hot granite. The grunts and groans and curses of the straining outlaws would have been funny if the situation had been different. I peered between the cracks in the granite.

They labored upward, passing south of me by about forty yards. I grimaced. "Not there," I whispered when I saw where the Papago was leading them. "Not up there."

The Indian hesitated. For a moment, it appeared my prayers were answered, for the Papago angled toward the trail leading to the rimrock, bypassing the hidden passage by twenty yards. At the last minute, he cut toward the buckbrush- and creosote-covered entrance.

"What the blazes!" I muttered. "I told you, not up there, blast you. Not up there."

But, sure as Daniel Webster beat the devil, that gang of border trash headed directly for the hidden passage.

Without hesitation, I leaped to my feet and made a mad dash into the loblollies to the north, trying to make as much noise as I could. The sharp rocks jabbed at the soles of my feet.

"Hey! There he is," came a shout from behind.

The still air erupted with gunshots. Slugs whined past my head and thumped into the pine boles through which I twisted and wound my way. The slope was steep, steep enough that a jasper could lose his balance and fall all the way to Tucson.

The sounds of gunfire carried to the valley. If the boys were smart, they'd gather their catch and hightail it back to the cave—if they were smart.

"Hurry. Don't let him get away."

The voices behind spread out, some moving up and others down, trying to cut off any flight except straight ahead.

My heart pounded in my chest, and my breathing grew ragged. Suddenly, something jerked at the flapping strips that was one of my sleeves. In the next moment, my arm burned, but I continued running, dodging, twisting through the pines and behind the junipers.

Ahead, the loblollies gave way to a sprawling patch of juniper, growing so close together their limbs and branches intertwined.

"There he is!" A gunshot punctuated the exclamation, and a slug smashed into the granite at my feet, splattering my calves with slivers of granite as it ricocheted into the desert.

I lowered my head and hit the juniper patch at full chisel in an effort to bull my way through. If I could pick up a few seconds on them, I just might gain enough time to find a hole and pull it in after me.

The limbs and branches clung to my arms, grabbed my shoulders, twisted around my legs, but I kept my legs pumping, forcing my lanky body through the junipers, knowing the hombres behind would be facing the same problem.

Suddenly, I burst out of the patch and cut sharply down the slope, hoping to skirt the jasper below.

Behind me, the owlhoots crashed through the juniper, yelling and cursing. Clenching my teeth, I forced my legs to pump harder. Without warning, I hit a patch of loose rock covered by a layer of dry pine needles and sprawled headlong down the slope.

I bounced off a loblolly and skidded to a halt behind a second one. I lay motionless, gasping for breath.

Far above, I heard my pursuers thundering through the underbrush. Quickly, I rolled onto my stomach and buried my head in the dry needles, trying to force my body into the ground.

Moments later, the sounds of pursuit began fading. With a groan, I climbed to my feet and headed down the mountainside, not quite sure what my next move would be.

Emerging from the loblollies, I paused at the top of a piñon-dotted ridge that descended to the desert floor. A shout behind me pushed me on down the ridge. Halfway down the ridge, a motion to my left halted me. I jerked around and grinned.

In the basin below, a dappled gray stood ground reined, staring up at me. My hopes soared, but I suppressed my excitement, fearful of spooking him.

Moving slowly behind the animal, I spoke softly. His ears perked forward. He took a step, then jerked his foreleg back. Balanced on his one sound front leg, he sidestepped around until he faced me. "Easy, boy, easy," I whispered.

I'd always had a knack with animals. This one was no exception. He stood quietly as I approached. Gently, I eased a finger around the halter and scratched his jaw. "Yeah, now. See, no one's going to hurt you. Easy, easy."

I glanced at his foreleg, unable to tell if it was broken or merely a sprain, but one fact was certain—no one would be riding this animal for a while.

Despite the pressing pursuit, I took care not to startle the gray. I loosened the cinch and pushed the double-rigged Texas saddle off, all the while keeping up a soft, crooning patter of words. Then I removed the halter and stepped back. "Okay, fella. You're on your own."

The gray whinnied and stumbled back a step or two. I bent over the saddle, frowning when I discovered the saddle gun was missing. I dug through the saddlebags, coming up with a Barlow knife, two ragged linsey-woolsey shirts, three tins of black powder, a crimping tool, and a chunk of lead. Whoever owned the gray built his own cartridges. That and a new lariat was all I could salvage from the discovery.

Throwing the saddlebags over my shoulder, I grabbed the lariat and backtracked, hoping to run across their horses. If I could spook them, or even better, steal the animals, I could hide them in the passage until we all mounted, and then we could make a wild burst for freedom.

I hesitated, grimacing. "Don't be a fool, Andy. Can't you see Mrs. Barton forking one of those cayuses down the side of a mountain?" I shook my head. No. My best bet was to spook 'em, run the animals clean down to Mexico.

So I moved quickly but silently along my back-trail, keeping my eyes and ears cocked for any sign of the horses and taking care to stay among the piñons and junipers. Overhead, the sun beat down, drying the air and baking my shoulders. Sweat stung my eyes, but there was no sign of the horses.

Maybe I was wrong. Could be those jaspers left their horses back to the north. I shook my head.

That didn't make sense. A chuckle came from my throat unbidden. Who could say? Maybe they did. Maybe the owlhoots wanted to stay away from the scene of their run-in with the rattlers.

Far above, the rimrock of the Baboquivaris protruded into a sky as blue as a robin's egg. White clouds, puffy and full, rolled past the jutting ramparts. A red-tailed hawk, wings spread, rode the updrafts unmoving, pinned to the sky.

Just about the time I decided to turn back, a horse whinnied. I dropped to my knee and peered through the branches of a small piñon, searching the foothills beyond.

I listened carefully, but all I heard was the rustle of the noonday wind rushing up the mountainside. Carefully, I eased forward, wondering if I had truly heard anything or if it was only my imagination.

Moments later, I heard another whinny. I froze.

Directly ahead of me in a narrow basin between two granite ridges, several ponies stamped and snorted, reins snugged around small piñons and junipers. I remained motionless, studying the animals, searching for a guard or sentry. No one appeared in the vicinity.

After a few more minutes of waiting and seeing not a soul, I breathed easier. They all must be back north, chasing me. I chuckled. ''Just keep chasing, fellers," I muttered, slipping down the side of the ridge to the ponies.

I planned to loop the horses together and lead them back south and up into another valley deep in the Baboquivaris, one not even the Papago could find. There was plenty of water and graze. We could then sit back and outwait the Comancheros. After they left, we'd ride into Tucson in style.

Just as I reached for the reins of the first pony, a harsh voice stopped me. "Hold it right there, cowboy." The sharp click of a cocking hammer told me the voice meant business.

Chapter Six

I didn't move a muscle. The hombre behind me came closer. I could hear his boots crunching the sand. My back was to the sun, and my shadow angled out to my left. His shadow appeared near mine. I tightened my fingers about the lariat.

"Drop them saddlebags," he growled. "But don't make no sudden moves."

Slowly, I raised my left hand and slipped my thumb under the saddlebags and let them slip off my shoulder. As they fell, I spun to the right and swung the lariat, ripping the six-gun from his hand.

"What the—"

Before he could move, I whipped the lariat back, slapping him across his bearded face. In the next instant, I shot a short hook into his jaw, and he fell like a poleaxed steer.

A gunshot echoed across the mountain slope and a slug shattered on a chunk of granite behind me.

I wheeled around. Four figures raced across the slope in my direction. Grabbing the saddlebags, I darted up the side of the mountain, seconds ahead of three screaming Comancheros and one leering Papago.

I hit a game trail that twisted through the loblollies and swung up a sharp incline. At the top of the incline, the rocky trail forked, the one to the right leading upward into a clutter of cabin-sized boulders, the other to the left where it bowed around a vertical wall of granite and back into a patch of juniper.

Shouts echoed up the mountain. "There! That trail! That's where he is."

"I'll get 'im, I'll get 'im."

Without hesitation, I cut down the left branch, around the ledge toward the juniper. Two steps later, I skidded to a halt.

Stepping out of the junipers twenty feet away, a bristling grizzly glared at me with his pig eyes. The hump on his back twitched, the sunlight reflecting off the silver tips. He growled and shook his massive head in quick, sharp jerks, slinging drooling saliva from his glistening fangs. I gulped. I could have sworn I saw his tonsils, if grizzlies have tonsils.

There comes a time when instinct forgets all about thinking, and that's what happened to me. No sooner had I skidded to a halt than I spun in midair and raced back along the trail as fast as my feet would carry me.

By the time I reached the granite wall in the trail, I heard the grizzly grunting and pounding after me. In another twenty feet, he would be on me.

Just past the plate, I spotted the trail leading up into the patch of boulders. I threw myself onto the trail and rolled behind a small juniper. In the same motion, I pulled my handgun.

But the grizzly, roaring and bellowing, shot around the plate, past the fork, and bolted on down the trail.

Moments later, a bedlam of gunfire and wild screams ripped the silence apart. The grizzly roared, and men cursed.

"Watch out!"

"Find your own tree. This is mine!"

"Yaaaa!"

I jumped to my feet and hustled up the mountain without wasting a second. Luck can stretch just so far, and I figured mine had been strung out to the breaking point.

Thirty minutes later, I slipped into the hidden passage and hurried back to the valley.

When I stepped out of the passage into the valley, I heard a whoop. Down below, Otsie treaded water in the middle of the lake and waved at me. John Edward, standing knee-deep in the cold water, grinned.

Grace, her hair undone and streaming down her back, looked up from where she sat on the edge of the lake.

I couldn't help smiling. Looked like life in the wild agreed with them.

Off to my left, the mouth of the cave was empty, but I knew Mrs. Barton and Marline Ray had to be inside.

Grace and the boys hurried to me, hurling one question right after another.

"Hold on, hold on." I nodded to the cave. "Everyone needs to hear this."

Once I had everyone situated in the cave, I paused and stared at each of them. "You're not going to like what I've got to tell you, but I don't want any squalling and crying." I glared at Mrs. Barton, who turned up her nose and sniffed.

"I mean it," I said. "We've got enough problems facing us without any of us breaking down."

Grace whispered. "Is it that bad?"

"Worse than you think." I nodded. "Those riders we saw are Comancheros."

Dora Barton's eyes bulged. She opened her mouth to scream, but immediately jammed her fist between her teeth and chomped down on her fingers. Marline Ray sobbed, then bit her lip.

I grinned weakly, trying to give them some reassurance, and quickly related all that had happened.

Grace squared her shoulders. "What are we going to do?"

"Hard to say. I wish I could say we just sit tight and they'll go away."

"Won't they? I mean, won't they go away?" Dora Barton's bottom lip quivered.

"No. They know we're here. I don't like upsetting you, Mrs. Barton, but you best understand that you and Grace and the children are worth several hundred dollars in gold to the right folks down in Mexico. Hombres like them out there won't walk away from that kinda money. They'll hang around here until they get what they want, or . . ." I hesitated.

"Or what, Andy?"

I looked down at Grace. "Or until we kill them."

Shock spread across their faces—blank, unbelieving shock.

"Sometimes, there's no choice. If I thought we

could hide out and they would finally leave, I'd say let's do it. But like I said, they know you're here."

Grace squeezed Otsie's hand. She drew a deep breath. "What do we do first?"

Dora Barton looked around in surprise at Grace. "You . . . you mean you condone this . . . this savage behavior?"

Grace stared out across the peaceful valley for several seconds. Slowly, tears welled in her eyes. She turned her gaze back to Mrs. Barton. "We, Otsie and me, we were down at the Carreta Mines because my husband, Otsie's pa, was reported missing six weeks ago. I learned that he was murdered over a drunken card game by two of the men he worked with and his body dropped into a bottomless pit deep in the mine. Officials dropped almost three thousand feet of rope into the pit without reaching bottom."

She paused and smiled sadly down at her son. Without taking her eyes off the small blond, she said, "Why don't you tell me what's savage, Mrs. Barton? Is it savage to murder for money? Or is it savage to kill to save your life? To be truthful, right now, I've got no compassion for those out there searching for us."

For the first time since I had the dubious privilege of knowing Mrs. Barton, she was speechless.

Grace looked back up at me. "What do we do first, Andy?"

I nodded to her, understanding why she had been so silent and depressed when we first met. "First, we'll tighten up our defenses in here. The boys and I will set a couple of traps." I slipped the saddlebags from my shoulder and handed them to Grace. "You and the others are going to build some exploding spears."

After gathering half a dozen shafts six feet long, I gave Grace the Barlow knife. "Here. Now, I'll show you what you have to do." I hesitated. "If you feel like it. I . . . I reckon you've been through a lot these last weeks."

Her fingers lingered on my hand when she took the Barlow. "Andy . . ." She smiled wanly. "Yes. Yes, I feel like it." She glanced at Dora Barton, who was looking on curiously. "But after what I said, I . . . I suppose you're both wondering why I'm not in mourning black."

The thought had popped into my head upon learning of her husband's death, but I didn't figure it was any of my business. "Not especially."

Dora Barton stepped closer and nodded. "Well, it *is* curious."

Grace's smile grew sadder. "Dev . . . Dev left me and Otsie five years ago . . . to make his fortune."

She shook her head and chuckled wryly. "Some fortune. Anyway, it got to be that he was simply a name I was married to. No birthday or Christmas presents for Otsie, not even a letter for me . . . for five years." She forced a smile. "The first word of him in that time was to say he was dead."

She paused and drew a deep breath. "So, you see, Mrs. Barton, I'm a widow who hasn't seen her husband in five years. So why should I mourn?" She turned back to me and held up the Barlow. "Now, what is it you want me to do?"

I explained what I wanted, to hollow the middle of the shaft to a depth of about four inches, after which we would pack it with black powder, then wedge one of my Colt cartridges into the hole.

When the spear was thrown and the primer in the cartridge struck granite, it would fire the cartridge which would then explode the small amount of black powder. Unfortunately, the quantity was not so great that anyone would be injured, but they would certainly be frightened. On the other hand, there was no telling where the slug would go.

With the remaining powder, we would build some bombs.

While the women worked on the spears, the boys and I cut several young pines. On the granite slope above the passage entrance, we constructed a frame-work on which we stacked rocks and small boul-

ders. I set the trip rope a few feet beyond the mouth
of the cave, far enough that the Comancheros would
not have time to flee back inside when they spotted
the falling rocks. Their only choice would be to race
down the trail, away from the landslide, and into
our next set of traps.

In several spots farther down on either side of the
trail, we tied sharpened sticks to thick limbs and
slender saplings, which we then cinched back in an
arc and fastened each with a trip rope.

I stepped back and looked upon our handiwork.
"Well, boys. We did a fair job."

Otsie nodded emphatically. "We sure did."

John Edward whistled. "I bet they'll run like all
get-out when they step into our traps."

"Probably will, boy," I said, taking time to study
him for a moment. Amazing what a couple of days
of hard work did to a growing boy. From a mama's
boy whining and crying to a sturdy young man facing what needed to be faced.

Back in the cave, I poured powder into the hol-
lowed spear shafts, removed a slug from my gun-
belt, and gingerly backed the primer out of the
cartridge so it would have a better chance of making
first contact with the granite. Then I wedged the
slug into the shaft, leaving the primer protruding.

The remaining black powder, I packed into two

tins, added a handful of rocks to each, and stuffed as much of the shirts into the tins as I could.

When I finished, I packed the bombs away in the saddlebags and stacked the spears against the wall. Unbuckling my gun belt, I handed it to Grace. "I'm taking the Brass Boy tonight."

No one argued, no one questioned. We had all accepted the fact that we had to fight back.

Grace set her jaw. "What are your plans?"

"Try to scare them if I can. There's six left. If I can run off one or two, that'll cut the odds on down—"

"I can help."

I jerked my head around at John Edward, who had risen to his feet and was staring me squarely in the eyes.

"I'm almost thirteen. I can help."

"John Edward!" Mrs. Barton exclaimed, grabbing his arm and yanking him down beside her. "You'll do no such thing."

He jerked away from her. "I can help, Ma."

"Me, too, Ma. Me, too." Otsie jumped to his feet, his face beaming with excitement. He jumped up and down in front of his stunned mother. "I want to help, too."

"And you will, boy, you will," I interrupted. "But I need both of you here."

A frown knit John Edward's brows.

"Come out here on the ledge. You, too, Otsie. I want to show you what you've got to do for me, why I need you both here." The boys followed, and the mothers came after them. Marline Ray remained inside, pouting or crying or whatever spoiled fourteen-year-olds do.

I pointed out the log. "You're going to have to move that if the Comancheros show up here in the valley."

Dora Barton snorted. "My boy can't move that heavy log by himself. He'll break his back."

"He won't have to. Otsie will help."

She sneered. "He won't be any help. Why, he's just a baby himself."

Otsie glared up at her. "I am not."

Grace grabbed his shoulder. "Hush. You know you don't talk to grownups like that."

"But Ma, she—"

I interrupted again. "Hush, boy. You, too, John Edward. Listen to your mothers, both of you."

Mortified, the boys glared up at me. I ignored their dagger looks, instead nodding to the pines below. "Down there, we'll find a thick log for the boys to use as a lever."

Otsie frowned. "What's a lever?"

"A lever helps you move something you couldn't move by yourself. I'll show you when we find one. Let's go."

*   *   *

Thirty minutes later, we returned with a pine ten feet long—our lever. After demonstrating how to place a small boulder as the fulcrum and where to set the lever, I let them practice moving the log.

John Edward grinned broadly. ''That's easy. Why, we could move two or three logs like this.''

''Yeah.'' Otsie grinned.

I cautioned them. ''Remember—if the Comancheros start up the path to the cave, roll this log off the trail, then hide back inside the cave, deep.''

Grace nodded. I looked at the boys. They grinned at me.

''Okay.'' I had fashioned a sling for the bundle of spears and one for the Brass Boy, both of which I slipped over my shoulder. Next I threw the saddlebags over my other shoulder and reached for the lariat. ''I'll be back later.''

Overhead, the sky was turning pink. Thin clouds drifted past, their bottoms almost red.

Instead of taking the hidden passage, I shinnied up a narrow chimney to the top of the bluffs surrounding the valley. I planned on moving south along the peaks of the Baboquivaris. At night from such a vantage point, I should be able to spot their campfire much easier.

By the time I reached the top of the canyon, the sun had dropped below the horizon. I crawled to the edge of the rimrock and stretched out on my stomach so I could peer out across the mountain slopes and into the desert.

Nothing.

I wiggled around to make myself comfortable. No sense in moving about until I had reason to move.

When the temperature dropped, a shiver ran over my bare arms. My ragged shirt didn't offer much protection against the chill.

Suddenly, back to the north, a tiny fire flickered in the encroaching darkness. "So there you are," I whispered, rising to my feet. I stared at the fire. "Well, boys, you better get some sleep while you can. You won't get any after I get there."

Chapter Seven

Moving carefully through the shadows and keeping to the needle-covered ground, I reached the slope above the camp within an hour. From where I crouched behind an ancient piñon, twisted by the wind and weather, I made out six figures around the fire.

From the cursing and laughter, I guessed they were trying to see how many bottles of Monongahela whiskey they could pour down their gullets. A dark object stretched across the fire, venison by the smell drifting up the slope to me. My mouth watered.

I glanced around, surprised they didn't have a sentry out, at the same time pleased they were so confident of their own safety. Obviously, they figured the rattlesnakes dropping into their midst the night before was an act of nature.

Like a strike of lightning, an idea flashed into my head. I chuckled. Maybe they needed to understand that two could play this game of hide-and-seek. I shook my head at the outrageous idea that had burst into my head and refused to back away.

Behind me, back to my left a few yards, a house-sized outcropping of granite protruded from the side of the mountain like a finger pointing at the sky.

I studied the camp below, then gauged the distance between the tip of the finger and the camp. Maybe a hundred yards apart on the slope, but, if the two were on flat ground, no more than twenty or thirty yards would separate them.

"Yeah," I muttered. "A jasper could stand up there and chuck rocks right down their gullet."

For a few moments, I fingered the tin bombs in the saddlebags, then decided to go with my first idea.

Silently, I climbed to the base of the outcropping and placed the lariat, saddlebags, and spears beneath a small juniper. I cut me a snake stick, and headed for the warm rocks on which the rattlesnakes were hunting.

"Yeah, boys," I whispered to the Comancheros as I pinned a five-foot rattler to the ground. "In about five minutes, those thick skulls of yours are going to realize that someone's out here playing games with you.''

Holding the rattlesnake in my left hand between my thumb and middle finger, I pressed my forefinger against the top of his spade-shaped head. He wrapped his sinuous body around my arm tightly and squeezed. Quickly, I climbed to the top of the outcropping and peered down the slope.

An unbidden chuckle sounded in my throat, and I shook my head in mischievous glee at the surprise that was about to come down on the heads and shoulders of those six hombres. I unwound the snake from my arm, grabbed him by his rattles, and in one motion, dropped his head and swung him by his tail, like a rock on the end of a rope.

After the third or fourth loop, I lobbed the twisting serpent in a broad arc through the night air, hoping I had gauged the distance accurately.

The moonlight picked up the dark, squirming shape rising into the night and abruptly dropping down through the pines. I lost sight of the rattler when he fell behind the treetops, but the sound of his heavy body crashing down through the limbs echoed through the silence.

I cut my eyes back to the camp. Seconds later, the campfire exploded, coals and sticks scattering in all directions.

Several puzzled, startled curses carried through the darkness.

"What the . . ."

"Hey! Who—"

Abruptly, the puzzled curses turned into maniacal screams of terror and fear. A shout ripped through the night. "Snake, snake, *snake!*"

Gunfire erupted. Orange bursts of flame leaped from muzzles. Sparks flew as slugs tore up the coals.

One owlhoot leaped to his feet and stumbled backward over his saddle. Without wasting time getting to his feet, he dug his heels in the ground and scooted backward on his rear into the darkness, all the while pumping slug after slug at the fire. Coals exploded left and right.

A second jasper turned and leaped over some boulders, managing to straddle a pine tree and knock himself senseless. He staggered backward, his head swiveling about on his neck, his legs rubbery. He turned to the fire, his eyes rolled up in his head, and he sank to the ground.

I doubled over in laughter.

Four fast shots jerked me up.

One Comanchero lay sprawled on his back, his head up, wildly firing his pistol between his spread legs and screaming at the top of his lungs.

Suddenly, his screams turned into a screech and

he grabbed his foot. "My toe, my toe! I shot off my big toe." He bounced around the camp on one foot, clutching the other with his hands, wailing and screaming.

During the commotion, I slipped back down the outcropping, picked up the saddlebags, and eased through the shadows toward the camp, hoping to find a hiding place within twenty or so yards. Fifty yards distant, I slipped into the shadows and waited for the Comancheros to return to camp. The last thing I needed was to stumble into one of them out here.

Slowly, they made their way back into camp, the Papago the last. He remained in the shadows at the edge of the camp, studying the darkness around them.

After rebuilding the fire, the Comancheros passed the bottle around again, replacing some of the bluster the snake had scared from them.

I made my way closer, crawling on my hands and knees through the shadows. I halted behind a loblolly and peered around the trunk. The camp was twenty yards away, close enough for me to hear their conversation.

The one who shot off his toe had yanked off his boot and was attempting to reattach his toe.

"That ain't gonna work, Lutie," one of the Comancheros observed drily. "Might as well wrap it up and satisfy yourself that you'll be limping around on one foot from now on.'' He laughed.

Lutie moaned. ''Shut up, you . . . you heathen.''

The third Comanchero spoke up. ''Where the Sam Hill you figure that there rattler came from?''

Tulsa Jack stood in front of the fire, staring up the slope.

''What I wanta know,'' replied the other Comanchero, ''is how did that rattler get up in the tree?''

Tulsa Jack snorted. ''Idiots. Rattlers don't climb no trees. Someone threw it at us—that jasper we was chasing this morning, that's who. That's all it could be.''

The two Comancheros looked at each other and shrugged. Lutie ignored the entire discussion. He was busy taking turns pouring whiskey first on his toe and then down his throat.

''I reckon if the truth was told, that's where them rattlers came from last night.''

Lutie looked up from his toe. ''What do you mean, Jack?''

Jack shook his head. ''What do you think I mean, you addle-brained ignoramus? I mean that jasper out there probably tossed them snakes down on us last night in the ravine. He's the one what caused Two-Bit to get snakebit.''

I arched my eyebrows. Tulsa Jack was no dummy. I'd best keep that in mind. I squatted deeper into the shadows, keeping my eyes on the Papago. If the Indian disappeared into the surrounding pines, I'd move. Otherwise, I'd stay right where I was until first chance I had to set off the bomb.

I slipped the tin from the saddlebags. About five inches square, it fit comfortably in my hand. I didn't figure I'd have any trouble tossing it twenty yards.

A few minutes later, the Papago squatted, his back to me.

It was time. Slowly, I cocked the Brass Boy. At the final click, the Papago stiffened. *Blast his sharp ears,* I thought furiously.

Without hesitation, I leaped to my feet and hurled the tin of powder toward the camp. While it was still in the air, I jerked the Brass Boy to my shoulder. The can bounced on the ground and slid toward the campfire.

I squeezed off a shot.

The tin exploded, a ball of orange flame fifteen feet across. Instantly, I raced back up the slope, wanting to retrieve the spears and lariat before the Comancheros collected themselves.

Shouts and curses echoed through the night. I threw the spears over one shoulder and grabbed the lariat.

A moment later, Tulsa Jack's guttural voice broke the silence. "Hey, hombre! You listening?"

I remained silent.

"I know you hear me out there. You best listen good. We'll run you down. You can bet on it. There's six of us, and when we catch you, we'll cut you up in small pieces. Smartest thing you can do if you wanta save your carcass is hightail it outta here. You wanta leave, then git, but if you stay, you're dead meat, that's what you are. You hear me?"

When he finished, I promptly answered him with a spear, which to my surprise, worked exactly the way I planned.

"What the . . . !" Tulsa Jack yelled when the spear exploded nearby. From the darkness below, a chorus line of orange flame spurted from their six-guns, aiming in the direction of the spear.

I hurled another spear, beyond the camp, but this one failed to detonate. "Blast," I whispered, pulling out another and aiming it at the camp, hoping to hit some rocks.

It must've hit right in the middle of the owlhoots, for instantly the orange flames turned in on themselves.

"Watch out, you bunch of slab-sided idiots!" shouted Tulsa Jack. "You almost hit me. You're gonna kill each other."

I settled down beneath the outcropping and watched the camp. Their conversation drifted up the slope.

"Gimme some whiskey," whined Lutie. "My toe's killing me."

One of the Comancheros laughed. "You ain't got no toe, Lutie. How can it be killing you?"

Lutie cursed his tormentor. "Just gimme the whiskey."

The first outlaw laughed again. "Here you are." He hesitated, then spoke to Tulsa Jack. "What are we going to do about that hombre up there?"

Jack snorted. "You wanta go out there in the dark with him, you go ahead."

"Why don't you send that stinkin' Injun? That's all he's good for."

"I'd send you first. Just shut up. That jasper up there ain't planning on killin' us. He had plenty of chances. No, he just wants to run us off, but he'll find out right fast, we ain't running."

Tulsa Jack raised his voice. "You hear me up there, cowboy? We ain't running. We're sticking. Come daylight, we'll track you down."

I shook my head. Tulsa Jack was one stubborn jasper, the kind that needed a singletree between the eyes to get his attention. I considered my weapons, trying to figure what could take the place of a singletree. One bomb, three spears, a lariat, and fourteen .44s in the Brass Boy. Not much of a club for someone like the hombre below, but what I had would have to do.

First, I decided to pester them some, keep 'em from sleeping. A jasper without sleep could be downright ornery, and stupid.

Behind the outcropping, the granite walls of the Baboquivaris were split with gaping fissures by which I scaled upward another couple of hundred feet to a wide ledge that swung around the side of the mountain upward to the rimrock, a retreat if I needed one. From this vantage point, the camp shrunk to the size of a washtub.

Shucking my gear, I squatted near the edge, studying the camp and the forest surrounding it. The mountainside was a sharp relief of silver moonlight dotted with black shadows. I paid careful attention to the talus slope below, the most obvious approach to my position.

The camp seemed to be settling down. I had to hand it to Tulsa Jack. He was a strong hombre, able to force his men to do his bidding after all I'd dumped on them tonight. Still, the night was young.

I picked up a rock about the size of a persimmon and chucked it out over the top of the pines toward the camp below.

The rock hit with a popping clatter.

The camp burst to life with shouts and curses.

"What the . . . !"

"Look out!"

I tossed another.

"Hey! Watch out! That almost hit me," yelled one of the Comancheros.

Immediately, I threw another.

Gunshots replied.

One slug whizzed overhead, ricocheting off the granite far above my head. I backed away from the ledge, preventing a stray slug from catching me, and tossed another, then leaned back and waited. Suddenly, an idea hit me. I peered into the darkness at the granite walls above. I grinned.

I jumped to my feet and made my way up the ledge to the rimrock. Boulders of various sizes spread over the plateau, several near the edge. After a few minutes, I found exactly what I wanted, a small boulder about four feet wide. It rested high on the rimrock overlooking the slope of talus below.

The boulder was solid, unmoving. I tried rocking it from each side, but it refused to budge. Then I remembered the lesson I'd given the boys a few hours earlier. Quickly, I slipped the three remaining spears from my shoulder and wrapped the lariat tightly around them, fashioning a lever by which I could move the boulder.

The spears bent as I applied pressure, but I managed to move the boulder enough to kick some rocks under it. Upon releasing the lever, the granite boulder failed to settle back into its original spot.

Now I could rock the boulder. I strained as I

pushed. The boulder moved, then rocked back. Quickly, I managed a rhythm, each time forcing the boulder farther onto its side.

Without warning, the unwieldy stone pitched onto its side. I threw my shoulder into the boulder, keeping the momentum going. It rolled over and over and suddenly dropped off the rimrock, hurtling through the air until it crashed into the talus like a cannon shot, sending the entire slope rumbling and tumbling down toward the camp, with the boulder leading the way.

Shouts came from below, but the roar of the landslide smothered them. Dust filled the night, blocking out the forest below. Through the dust, the campfire glimmered faintly, then disappeared.

The squeal of a frightened horse cut through the rumble.

Moments later, the night grew silent.

Chapter Eight

Curses echoed up the mountain.

I grinned and settled down behind a juniper to watch the action below. Slowly, the dust settled, but the night was too dark to make out any detail, so I closed my eyes and laid my head on my arms. After resting a while, I would slip down and see what had taken place.

I awakened with a start. The sun was rising. I muttered a curse and blinked the sleep from my eyes while I tried to focus on the mountainside below. With a sigh of relief, I relaxed.

Six figures crouched around a small fire far below.

Unfortunately, the loblollies surrounding the camp had diverted most of the rockslide.

For a moment, I considered potshotting them while they squatted over coffee, but I decided against it. I'd much rather watch them than hide from them. Maybe last night had convinced the owl-hoots to back away, find some victims some other place.

But even as I considered the possibility, I knew it was too farfetched. The sobering realization that Tulsa Jack and his band of Comancheros were not about to give up was slowly taking a firm, unshakable hold in my brain.

I stared at the Brass Boy, hefting it in my hands, absently testing the balance of the rifle. I didn't want to kill anyone, but from the looks of Tulsa Jack and his band of cutthroats, they might very well not give me any choice.

At that moment, a whisper of motion far to the right on the mountain slope caught my attention. I strained to pick up the source of the movement, but the rising sun cast bright rays across the slope, intensifying the shadows, making them deeper, darker.

Back to my left, the Comancheros still huddled about the fire. Abruptly, the Papago stood and peered to the south, in the same direction as the movement I had spotted. I turned my gaze back to the mountain slope, searching for anything out of place. Nothing.

Whatever I missed, the Papago spotted, for he swung onto his pony and raced across the slope, weaving through the loblollies.

What in blazes had stirred him up?

I cursed. What was out there that lit such a fire under his feet? What was it that I couldn't see?

My blood chilled.

Two small heads stuck up out of a patch of buck-brush and creosote.

Otsie! And John Edward!

I leaped to my feet.

Without hesitation, I jerked the Brass Boy to my shoulder and fired. The Papago's horse stumbled, causing the two-hundred-and-sixteen-grain slug to pass just in front of the Indian instead of catching him in the side where I aimed. The slug slammed into the saddle horn, and the impact knocked the pony off balance, sending him and his rider sprawling headlong across the mountain slope.

At the shot, both boys leaped from the creosote and raced down the mountain.

"No!" I shouted. "Up here, up here." But the wind carried my voice back across the rimrock, away from the valley below.

The Papago hit the ground and rolled to his feet, risking a look over his shoulder in my direction before pounding down the mountain after the boys. Before I could snap off another shot, he disappeared among the loblollies.

Back at the camp, four riders spurred their ponies after the Papago, vanishing back into the pines before I could throw my rifle to my shoulder.

I groaned. Unless the boys found themselves a heap of luck, their gooses were cooked, which meant the Comancheros would have us just where they wanted us. First, they would try to reach me through the boys. When that didn't work, they'd force the younkers to show them the hidden passage.

And when the owlhoots discovered the passage . . .

I tried not to think about that. There were only five Comancheros left, six counting Lutie, the outlaw with one big toe, and he remained in camp. I clenched my jaw. I could handle five and a half border bandits like them. If I couldn't, then there was always White Eye, my Apache brother. I hadn't forgotten how to send smoke.

Gathering my gear, I hurried back down the ledge, then slid down the chimney to the talus and scooted into the undergrowth. Remaining among the juniper and piñon along the rocky slope butting against the base of the granite walls, I eased back to the north, hoping to come into the Comanchero camp from the opposite side.

I figured my chances of rescuing the boys would be a lot better once they were in the outlaw camp rather than stumbling across them wandering about the foothills. In camp, everyone would be congregated, in one place.

Shouts came from below, scattered from the ridges to the desert. From the movement, I guessed the boys had so far managed to evade the Comancheros.

I skirted the camp. From a distance, Lutie appeared to be sleeping, passed out from too much Old Orchard probably, but I didn't want to take a chance on being spotted. I moved northeast, down the slope, looking for a refuge from which I could watch the camp.

In the middle of one ridge, several granite plates protruded, pushing the soil between them upward almost twenty feet above the surrounding ground, forming a knoll covered with a bunchgrass and a thick stand of scrawny piñons that reminded me more of fence posts than trees. Animal trails led between the jutting plates up into the piñons, offering not only several exits but a view of the camp from the crest of the knoll.

Squirming around in the middle of the piñons, I wormed out a small nest in the bunchgrass where I could watch the camp. I waited and listened, turning one option after another over in my mind. Each plan I considered had a flaw, one serious enough to get one or both of the boys killed.

Finally, I came to the conclusion that I would have to wait and see what opportunity presented itself, and then act as quickly as I could.

The shouting faded away.

The noonday sun beat down. I shifted my position into the feeble shade of the angular piñons. Down below, the camp was silent. Lutie remained sprawled on his back. A few tendrils of smoke drifted into the clear air from the bed of coals. Even the ever-present aroma of coffee no longer hung on the air. From the pines came the thin *ssst, ssst* song of the golden-crowned kinglet, and the light breeze whispered a soft hum as it ran its delicate fingers through the treetops.

I stared at my hand, caked with dust. I wiggled my fingers, watching curiously as the tendons and ligaments on the back of my hand stood out like the bones on a skeleton. Scarred and gnarled from hard work, my hands were a perfect example of the rest of my lanky frame, thin to the point of starvation, tough as the heart of a red oak, and unyielding as the ramparts of the Baboquivaris.

Those qualities had caused me a heap of trouble in my life. Sometimes, I wondered if there was any other way in this life to get by without having to constantly battle. More often than not, when I lay down at night, I was so weary I was asleep before my head touched my saddle. But I slept the peaceful sleep of a clear conscience.

The clatter of hooves against rock jerked me back to the present. I peered in the direction of the commotion.

A few minutes later, four horses emerged from the loblollies, followed by the Papago pushing a boy ahead of him.

Otsie!

I squinted, trying to find John Edward, but he was nowhere in sight. He had escaped. I looked back over the foothills behind the Comancheros. John Edward, the mama's boy, was by himself out there.

"Blast," I muttered. I blew through my lips. Now when I rescued Otsie, we still had to worry about John Edward. Out of the proverbial frying pan into the fire.

The Papago had Otsie by the collar, but the squirming, screaming boy wasn't going easy. He fought every inch of the way.

To my surprise, the Papago had a grin on his face, not of cruelty, but something akin to admiration for the young boy's determination and fight.

But that didn't surprise me when I pondered it. Courage and determination, refusal to accept defeat, these were qualities that transcended enemies and age, that were to be admired by even a jasper's mortal antagonist. In the early generations of the native American, the Indian, the culture had developed such a natural philosophy, one that admired courage and despised cowardice, among mankind as well as animal. The belief passed from father to son.

But Tulsa Jack didn't see the situation that way. When he dismounted, he strode back to Otsie and the Papago. He shoved the Papago away and slapped the six-year-old across the cheek, knocking him to the ground.

My muscles bunched, but I held back. Now was not the time to make my move. "Just wait, Jack," I muttered. "You'll get the chance to pick on someone your size. Let's see how you are then."

The commotion awakened Lutie who, ignoring his cohorts, painfully unwrapped his foot and poured some more Old Orchard over it, after which he dumped a goodly amount down his throat.

"You best go easy on that rotgut," growled Tulsa Jack. "You ain't no use to me drunk."

"What the Sam Hill, Jack. It hurts. You ain't never had no toe shot off." His tone took on a whining note. "I might not ever be able to walk again. I heard up in Dodge one time about this hombre who lost a toe and couldn't never stand up again."

"Bull." Tulsa Jack snorted and grabbed the bottle from Lutie. "You got the backbone of a snake. Stop whining. So you got a toe shot off. You're still alive, ain't you?" He hurled the half-full bottle into the loblollies. "You make me sick to my belly. You ain't on the little end of the horn yet."

Lutie cried out and reached out his arms as the bottle flew over his head.

In the meantime, the other Comancheros stirred up the fire and put coffee on to boil. I figured they would settle down for a spell, long enough to guzzle some coffee and fry up some bacon or venison.

To my surprise, Tulsa Jack gestured to the Papago. He whispered to the Indian for several seconds, pointed to the foothills, then to the rimrock and laid his hand on his knife, an Arkansas toothpick.

The Papago hesitated.

Jack doubled his fist and drew back his arm.

With a curt nod, the Papago turned and disappeared back into the forest.

I grimaced. The Indian was going back for John Edward and me, one or the other, or both.

With no time to waste, I looped the lariat over my shoulder and scooted down the back of the knoll, keeping it between me and the camp. I looked around in frustration. The Baboquivaris extended north to south for miles. John Edward could be in almost any of the foothills, and now the Papago was out there also.

Glancing back in the direction of camp, I decided to swing back east to the edge of the desert and then south, wide around the camp, and come in from the southwest. Then I would scoot up high on the slope, directly between the camp and the entrance to the hidden passage. Even if I couldn't find John Edward, I would be putting myself in a position to ambush the Comancheros once they got their information on the hidden passage from Otsie.

I moved quietly, ghosting from one shadow to the next, silent as a spider skittering over his web.

John Edward appeared so suddenly, I stopped in my tracks. I had crossed three ridges and paused behind a weatherworn piñon on the fourth when I saw him coming out of the loblollies on the slope above.

His name leaped to my lips. Just as I stood to wave, a dark figure emerged from the undergrowth below and hurried up the sandy bed to the crest of the ridge. The Papago.

John Edward hadn't seen the Indian. I wanted to shout, but with the Papago between us, all I would be doing was warning the Indian. Maybe he hadn't spotted John Edward despite the boy's noisy and clumsy efforts to escape.

When John Edward reached the ridge, he turned

down the spine, weaving between the piñons, heading for the desert. Maybe he'd remembered my instructions about heading northeast to reach Tucson.

Below, the Papago froze. He looked around, searching for the source of the noise above. He dropped into a crouch, his braids almost touching the ground.

I grimaced. He'd spotted the boy.

My brain raced. Now what? Gunshots would bring the others, maybe get one of the boys hurt.

Taking a deep breath, I headed back up the ridge, into the loblollies from where I would be able to spot the Papago when he and John Edward came out of the foothills. If I could find the right spot, I could waylay him.

John Edward made it easy for me.

Before I reached the loblollies, I heard a shout back down in the foothills. Moments later, quick as a jackrabbit, John Edward darted from behind a patch of creosote and zigzagged for the loblollies.

I stepped from behind a pine and waved. He spotted me and I waved harder, signaling him to hurry. As he raced toward me, I tossed the loop of my lariat around a broken limb and laid the rope on the ground across a wide gap through which John Edward was heading. I crouched behind a boulder.

Just as he reached me, he slowed, grinning. I waved him on. "Keep going."

He hesitated, but when he looked over his shoulder and saw the Papago less than thirty yards behind, he burst into an all-out run.

I hoped the Papago wouldn't see the rope. I'd had no time to kick pine needles over it.

To my surprise, John Edward slid to a halt and turned to face the Indian. He stuck his thumb to his nose and waggled his fingers. "Yah, yah, yah."

The Papago saw nothing but the boy and a blazing anger.

Just as he got even with me, I yanked the rope. It jerked up and caught him under his chin. His head and torso stopped, but his feet kept going, circumscribing a complete loop about the rope, bringing him smashing down on his face.

Before he could move, I jumped him, planting a knee in his spine. John Edward came racing up as I yanked the Papago onto his back. I pulled my knife and jabbed the tip under his chin. I lapsed into the Apache dialect, with which most Papagos were familiar.

"I am called Bear Claw, son of Horse of Water, brother to White Eye. The Papago is no more than the leavings of dogs, not worthy of one drop of sweat from the Apache."

He glared at me, defiant, insolent. My words were no more than water over pebbles to him. I knew that one day, one of us would probably be forced to kill the other. I pressed the point of the knife harder. A bubble of blood appeared around the point. Perhaps I should have gotten it over with, but life was too valuable. I couldn't kill a helpless man.

On the other hand, I couldn't turn him loose to return to the camp. And I couldn't trust his word. A Comanchero's first love was money. He'd lie, cheat, kill to get it.

The only choice I had was to tie him to a tree and hope he'd stay until I could free Otsie. "Come on. Get to your feet." I grabbed him and pulled him to his feet.

His hand flashed. I ducked, but my head exploded as he struck me a glancing blow with a chunk of granite. I fought to remain conscious, but a black wave threatened to engulf me.

A sharp scream pushed back the darkness.

He leaped at me, knife drawn, his arm coming forward.

I threw up my arm, knocking his aim askew, but the razor edge caught my shoulder, slicing through the skin. I rolled to the left, pinning his knife under me.

He yanked and grunted, trying to free the knife, but I swung a gnarled fist and caught him on the point of the chin. He went limp. I rolled to my feet and kicked his knife away.

John Edward approached tentatively, his eyes

wide. He had witnessed much in the last few days, enough to shock any boy, much less a mama's boy. "Are . . . are you all right, Mr. Stonecipher?"

"Yeah." My shoulder burned and I could feel the warm blood running under my arm and trickling down my side.

Jerking the Papago to his feet, I lashed him face forward to a pine, stretching his arms around the trunk. I pressed his palms together and tied not only his wrists, but also bound thumbs to thumbs and fingers to fingers.

After I gagged the Indian, John Edward said, "They caught Otsie."

"I know."

"Are we going to get him?"

I looked down at the twelve-year-old. He had changed the last day or so. I couldn't quite put my finger on it, but he had changed.

"Are we, huh?"

"Yeah, son. We're going to get him."

Chapter Nine

Taking the Papago's gun belt and knife, I turned up the slope toward the hidden entrance, then hesitated. What if the Comancheros spotted us? We'd lead them right into the valley.

We paused in a copse of piñon. I peered across the mountainside toward the Comancheros' camp, cursing because of the time I was wasting. I had to take the boy back to the valley. If I didn't, the women might become so worried, they'd come out too.

And that's all I would need. Two women and a spoiled girl wandering the mountains. That sure wouldn't work.

There was no choice. I doubled back and headed

south, planning on skirting the slopes of talus and making my way up through the loblollies and piñons, then scaling the mountain to the rimrock. From there, we'd travel through the peaks to the valley where I would use the lariat to lower John Edward into the valley.

Hurrying through the underbrush, I muttered, "What the blazes possessed you boys to leave the valley?" Before John Edward could explain, I continued, growing angrier by the second. "I reckon that's the most all-fired, hammerheaded play I ever seen. You know you left the women up there all alone."

John Edward remained silent. I figured he felt bad, ashamed, and he should have. No one goes off and leaves a woman by herself, not even a boy. There was no excuse for such a shameful act. I grew silent.

Later, when we reached the base of the mountains, I tossed him the end of the lariat. "Loop that under your arms and follow me up the mountain."

He nodded silently, quickly knotting the rope.

As we ascended the mountain, I kept glancing back to the north, wondering if I could see the Comancheros' camp, but the talus slope leading to the hidden entrance was beyond my sight. I grimaced, and climbed faster.

Once on the rimrock, we broke into a trot toward the valley. Fifteen minutes later, we pulled up.

I gave him the Papago's gun belt and knife. "Here. You'll need this. You got two six-guns and plenty of cartridges now. I'll lower you here. You get down there and keep the women calm. And stay with them. You hear?"

He nodded, fully shamed. "I . . . I hear." He looked up at me hopefully.

I knew what he wanted, for me to tell him that what he had done was all right, to give him back some sense of worth.

At twelve years, the top of his head came to my shoulder. "Look, boy. I want you to understand something. You boys going off and leaving the womenfolk was a sin to Crockett, to any man of the West. But you are a boy, and as such, I suppose you're entitled to one mistake." I fixed him with a cold, hard stare. "You made your one. Don't make no more. Out here, one mistake can kill you."

Despite my harsh words, a faint grin played over his lips. He nodded. "Yes, sir. Don't worry. I won't."

After a moment, I returned his grin. "Okay, now here's what I want you to do. Once you let the women know what's going on, once you get them calmed down, you go to the entrance of the passage. Set yourself down behind the creosote and buckbrush and keep an eye out on the slope below. Never can tell when I might need you.''

His eyes grew brighter and his chest pumped up. He nodded eagerly. "Yes, sir. Don't worry. I'll take care of the women. I surely will.''

"And watch out for the trip rope. You don't want to bring that pile of rocks tumbling down on you.''

"No, sir . . . I mean, yes, sir. I'll watch out.''

After lowering John Edward and retrieving the lariat, I backtracked to the fissure up which we had climbed earlier. I descended recklessly, rushed for time, hoping to catch the Comancheros before they broke camp. A rock rolled from under my foot, and I lost my balance. The next thing I knew, I was in the middle of space, heading down.

At the last second, I managed to grab the base of a wiry mesquite growing from a narrow crack in the side of the mountain.

For long seconds, I dangled over a fifty-foot drop, clinging with my left hand while I scrambled to dig my fingers into a cleft in the granite so I could pull myself back into the narrow fissure. Sweat beaded on my forehead. I felt my fingers slipping.

I clenched my teeth, and with a straining groan, dug my fingers into the fissure and pulled myself back to safety. After catching my breath, I continued my descent, this time slowly and carefully. I was no use to anyone with a broken leg or neck.

Luck must have decided to pony up my share because Otsie and the Comancheros were still in camp when I reached the knoll; however, after I settled in and managed a good look at the camp, my blood ran cold.

Luck had played no part in keeping the Comancheros in camp. It had been all Otsie. The evidence was obvious. His cheeks were red, and his chin and chest were splashed with blood dripping from his nose.

Tulsa Jack and his band of scum had been knocking the boy around, but Otsie had kept his mouth shut. I was both proud and outraged, a mixture of emotions that could cause me to take some reckless steps.

As I looked on, Jack slapped the boy again, sending him spinning to the ground where he lay unmoving. I jerked the Brass Boy Henry to my shoulder, ready to send two hundred and sixteen grains of lead through Tulsa Jack's brain. If he touched the boy one more time, he was dead.

Jack hesitated, his arm raised. He stared down at the boy and shook his head. ''What the tarnation? Beatin' on this kid is like kicking a tree stump.'' He looked up at the rimrock and shook his head. I had the strange feeling he was having second thoughts about the women and children. My hopes soared.

"Hold off, Jack," said the Comanchero named Snag. "Night's coming. Let the younker go hungry tonight. He'll be talking in the morning, I guarantee it."

Lutie looked up from his toe. "Looks who's talking. Why, you ain't never had nothing to do with no children. How do you reckon to know what they'll do?"

Defensively, Snag shot back, "I was a younker myself once. I oughta know."

A second Comanchero rose to his feet and snorted. He peered into the encroaching night. "What happened to the Injun? He's been gone a powerful long time."

"Who cares?" Tulsa Jack growled and squatted by the fire. "He ain't done much Injunning for us anyway. We're better off without him." He remained silent for a moment, then grunted. "I oughta shoot that red savage."

Otsie rolled over and slowly sat up, his hand pressed against his cheek. He glared defiantly at Tulsa Jack, who returned the look with a murderous one of his own. The Comanchero leader nodded to the outlaw who had been scanning the mountainside for the Papago. "Tie this kid up. I don't want no trouble from him tonight."

"Aw, he ain't going nowhere, Jack."

Tulsa Jack's face darkened. His bearded jaw twitched. "Shut your mouth. Do what I said. Tie this kid up."

"Awright, awright. Don't have a conniption fit."

"And make sure he ain't got no Barlow in his pocket. I don't want him cutting them ropes tonight."

Otsic shook his head. "I don't got a knife."

"Shut up, kid." The Comanchero jerked Otsie onto his side and jammed his hand in the boy's pocket. "I'll look for myself."

Otsie struggled, but the outlaw dropped his knee on the boy's side, pinning him to the ground. "I said, stop jumping around, or I'll hurt you bad."

The other Comancheros looked on, grinning wickedly.

"Looks like you need some help there." One laughed.

"I don't need nothing." He grunted and pulled his hand from Otsie's pocket. "I... hey, what's this?" He rolled something between his fingers and held it up to the light from the campfire. "Why, I'll be hornswoggled." He peered hard at the object in his hand. "This looks like—" He looked up at

Tulsa Jack. "It is. That's what it is, Jack. Gold. It's gold."

I closed my eyes and groaned.

The Comanchero leader frowned. "Huh?"

"Yeah. Hey, yeah, yeah. Gold. The kid had a chunk of gold in his pocket."

Tulsa Jack dropped his cup and reached for the gold. "Let me see that."

All I could do was shake my head and roll my eyes. I cursed myself. I should have pointed out the narrow ravine at the rear of the valley and insisted the boys stay out of it, but instead I'd just hoped they wouldn't discover it. I should have known better. Stick two curious boys in an enclosed area like the valley, and they'll explore every inch.

I blew through my lips. No sense in worrying about it now. What was done was done.

Jack held the gold close to the fire. "It sure enough is gold," he said, looking up at the Comanchero who found it. "A chunk the size of a marble." He tossed it up and down in his palm, testing its weight. "Heavy, too. Probably worth a hundred dollars."

Lutie stopped massaging his foot. "A hun—"

"We're rich!" shouted the second Comanchero. "Rich!"

All five of the Comancheros huddled over the pebble of gold. Otsie scooted slowly away from the group, his head revolving on his neck as he tried to find a route of escape.

I gave three short whistles, the signal I had given them back in the valley before I left that first day.

Otsie heard me. He jerked his head around in an effort to pinpoint my location.

Dusk had settled over the mountain, blurring figures, running objects together. Taking a gamble, I stood and waved the Henry over my head, at the same time giving three more short whistles.

I dropped to my knees.

Otsie spotted me. In the next instant, he darted from the camp in my direction. At the same time, I burst from the knoll, heading up the slope through the loblollies. He angled off to meet me.

Behind him, the Comancheros leaped to their feet.

"Catch that kid!" Tulsa Jack's guttural voice echoed across the slopes.

"I'll wear his rear end out!" shouted another Comanchero.

Darkness was settling in. Otsie and me missed each other in the loblollies. I heard the pounding of feet coming in my direction, so I pressed up against a pine. As the figure rushed past, I swung the muzzle of the Henry like an ax, deliberately holding back, not out of fear of injuring the Comanchero but because I couldn't afford to bend the barrel.

I caught him right between the eyes with enough force that he dropped like a bag of oats.

Immediately, I ducked back behind the pine, listening to the footsteps rattling the dry pine needles and clattering over the scattered rocks.

Where was the boy? Which set of footbeats was his? I tried to discern a difference between footsteps, but it was impossible.

Then I heard some behind me that seemed softer, tentative.

Just before I stepped out, a voice echoed from up the slope. "I got 'im, Jack. I got 'im."

Before I could move, a large dark figure stepped past me and paused. I froze, unable to tell if he was looking at me or the voice in the distant. I watched his arms for any threatening movement.

He shouted. When I heard the guttural voice, I knew the hombre in front of me was Tulsa Jack. "Hold 'im. Tight."

Immediately, Jack headed in the direction of the voice. I relaxed and sagged back against the pine. Despite the chill of the mountain air, sweat rolled down my forehead and stung my eyes. I dragged the back of my hands across my forehead.

Jack stalked through the loblollies. I remained motionless, waiting for him to put enough distance between us so I could slip back into the knoll safely.

Once snug in my hideaway, I could set up another plan to rescue Otsie.

Voices rolled down the slope. I peered into the darkness. Beyond the loblollies on a moonlit slope, dark silhouettes, three of them, traipsed across the rocky soil. A small silhouette stumbled ahead of them. I clenched my fists, aching because of the punishment the boy was taking, but Otsie would be even worse off if I let them take me.

Quickly, I tallied bodies. One Comanchero lay back in the loblollies where I had coldcocked him. Counting him, and the Papago tied to the tree, and Lutie in camp with his shot off toe, those three silhouettes with Otsie had to be Jack and the remaining Comancheros.

I grinned and pushed away from the tree. If I hurried, I could reach the knoll before they reached camp. Before I had taken two steps, a rustling of needles off to my left caused me to drop to my knee beside a loblolly.

I peered into the darkness around me, trying to pick up the silhouette of the source of the faint sound. The night grew silent as a mute, still as a corpse. Holding my breath, I slowly lowered myself to my belly.

Long seconds passed. Then the rustling sounded again. Without moving my head, I cut my eyes in the direction of the whispery movement. The sound grew louder, more distinct.

Who in the blazes could it be? I'd accounted for everyone. The Papago, Lutie, the unconscious owlhoot, Tulsa Jack, and the remaining Comancheros. So who, or what, was creeping through the loblollies toward me?

The sound grew louder. I slipped my knife from its sheath, just in case. The movement angled to my right. Slowly, I turned my head. Needles, pressed into my cheek, fell when I raised my head.

The sound stopped.

I squinted into the darkness. *Blast!* It was like staring into a bottle of schoolroom ink. I held my breath. Long seconds passed. I stared hard, and suddenly I had the eerie feeling that whoever or whatever was out there was staring back at me. I gulped.

A musky odor filled my nostrils. I stiffened. Snake? Then I relaxed. No, not a snake. Whatever this was had feet.

Long seconds passed, then a soft snort, and the movement continued, passing on my right and heading up the slope toward the rocky clearing behind me.

I craned my neck, hoping to pick up a silhouette as the mysterious source highlighted itself against the moonlit background of the clearing.

Then I saw it. I grinned sheepishly. A deer. That

was all it was, a deer. As I watched, the small animal made its way toward the clearing, pausing on the edge of the loblollies to search ahead for any sign of danger.

The deer—a buck, for now I could make out the small rack on his head—arched his head to the left, peering in the direction Tulsa Jack had disappeared with Otsie.

I pushed myself to my feet and sheathed my knife. I took a deep breath and breathed a sigh of relief.

My head exploded, and I felt myself falling forward into a dark night filled with thousands of brilliant stars.

Chapter Ten

A sharp pain in my side jarred me awake. I tried to ignore it, to slip back into the bliss of dreams, but the stabbing sharpness cut through the fog of unconsciousness in which I drifted. I opened my eyes and stared at the firelit ground inches from my eyes. Shards of silvered granite gouged my face and chest.

The pain struck again. I winced and moaned.

"Hey, Jack. He's comin' around."

I clamped my eyes shut and kept them closed. My brain was addled, but not so much that I couldn't figure out their plans for me when I awakened.

"Come on, hombre. Wake up." The Comanchero

116

slammed the toe of his boot into my ribs. I moaned, but kept my eyes closed. "Come on, you spavined broomtail. Wake up." He kicked me again.

I almost screamed from the pain. It felt like he'd cracked a rib.

"Leave 'im alone," Tulsa Jack growled. "We'll take care of him in the morning. Besides, I want you to ride back to the train." The two Comancheros walked away. I strained to hear, but the chirp of the crickets and cries of the night birds drowned their whispers.

The pain continued, slowly subsiding until I finally dozed. My slumber was fitful, interrupted each time I moved, aggravating my ribs. Deep in the jumbled images of my subconscious, I visualized payback for my ribs. Face after gloating face, I stomped. And each time, my dream ended with Tulsa Jack.

Just after 2:00 A.M., I awakened. The fire was low. I eased my head around until I could see the camp. When I did, I froze. The Papago slept directly across the fire from me. So that was where the other silhouette came from. That's why I had been fooled. The Papago had escaped and returned. I peered around the camp. One of the Comancheros was missing. Was it the one I'd laid out with the muzzle of my Henry?

No. One with a swollen nose slept near the fire,

his mouth open, his throat gargling with drainage. Even in the faint glow of the dying flames, I could see the black and yellow bruises across his face.

I moved my head slowly, pinpointing each member of the gang. Yeah, one was missing. And then I remembered that when I had awakened earlier, Tulsa Jack had sent a Comanchero back to the train.

A grimace twisted my face. You didn't have to be schoolteacher-smart to figure out what was back at the train. More Comancheros.

Next to me, Otsie slept, a deep, silent slumber despite his hands tied behind his back and his ankles bound up like a gunnysack. I glanced around the slumbering camp once again. I had to get the boy out of here. I could take anything the Comancheros tried with me, but the boy, Otsie—I closed my eyes. I didn't want to think about what they would do to him.

My hands were tightly bound. I twisted and yanked, but the rope refused to give. I jerked with one hand, hoping to slip it from the loop. A sharp pain bit into my forearm. I winced.

Warm blood oozed down my arm. I had slashed it on one of the granite shards mixed with the thin soil of the mountain. Suddenly, I knew how I could free us. Quickly, I worked a thin sliver of granite free and ran my finger over the edge. I grinned. Like a knife. This would be a snap.

Easing closer to the boy, I whispered, "Otsie. Wake up. You hear me? Wake up!"

He moaned and squirmed.

I lay motionless, my ears tuned for any sound from the sleeping Comancheros behind us. All I heard was a strange mixture of snoring and gargling.

"Otsie." I popped my head forward, striking him in the middle of the back. "Wake up."

He jerked. "Huh? Huh?"

"Shhh. Be quiet. Don't move."

I've got to hand it to the boy. He behaved a lot more grown up than a six-year-old.

"Okay," he replied, his voice barely audible.

"We're getting out of here. Stick your hands out behind your back. I'll cut the ropes. You untie your feet while I cut my own. When we're both free, we'll sneak out of here, but be quiet."

He nodded.

I rolled over and found the ropes binding his wrists. I began sawing, and sawing, and sawing. My fingers grew raw. *So much for a snap,* I told myself after ten minutes. Pausing, I touched my fingertips to the rope. I suppressed a groan. We still had more than halfway to go.

Broken Nose rolled over. A paroxysm of coughing seized him, disturbing the camp. I closed my eyes and lay motionless.

"Shut up," Tulsa Jack growled.

The Comanchero sat up and whined, "It ain't my fault, Jack. I can't breathe."

Tulsa Jack rolled over and pulled his blanket over his shoulders. "Then go off somewhere else and sleep. Just stop bothering me, or I'll put a hole in the middle of that plug-ugly face and stop the whining myself."

A few assenting grunts punctuated Tulsa Jack's response. Broken Nose groaned and lay back.

Slowly, the camp grew silent.

Gingerly, I began sawing once again, keeping my eyelids cracked so I could watch the camp.

Thirty minutes later, his ropes fell apart.

"Okay," I whispered. "Don't sit up. Bend over and untie your feet."

Then I started sawing on my own bonds, figuring on another forty-five minutes. I glanced upward, but I couldn't find a star that gave me the time. About 4:00 A.M., I guessed.

Suddenly, I felt fingers on my ropes.

Otsie was loosening my hands. He was small enough that in the dark, he was hard to see behind me. Moments later, my hands were free.

I listened as he scooted around, and then I felt him working on my ankles.

Another ten minutes and they were free.

"Just lie still for a moment," I whispered.

"Okay."

"If we get separated, you've got to go on your own. You think you can find the hidden entrance by yourself?"

His reply was soft and frail. "Y . . . yes."

"You'll have to watch out for rattlers on the slope. They like the warm rocks."

"Okay."

"If we get separated, you keep the women and children in the valley." I hesitated. I didn't know what else to say. I couldn't tell him to outwait the Comancheros. Those border renegades would never leave, not until they found the source of the gold they'd discovered in Otsie's pocket.

My only hope was to call in my Apache family, and I cringed at the thought. They had enough problems of their own without mixing into mine. Still, in an emergency—

"Now listen, Otsie. Listen carefully," I whispered over my shoulder, still facing the camp. "If we get separated, and I don't get back in a day or two, build a large fire in the valley. Once it gets real hot, throw on green limbs and wet leaves. The smoke will bring my Apache brother. He'll help you get back to Tucson."

For a few seconds, Otsie remained silent. Then in a low voice, he replied, "I will. Don't worry."

A strange feeling came over me then, one unlike

I'd ever before experienced. I felt a liking for this boy. I wouldn't mind taking him along on a bear hunt, or some winter traplines.

The feelings puzzled me, for in the past, I never liked being around people. Now, I was with a six-year-old sprout who I truly enjoyed being around. Strange.

"Okay, now slow and easy, work back to the underbrush."

Sweat beaded on my forehead. I bunched my muscles, ready to leap to my feet if any of the Comancheros awakened, but they slept the sleep of children. How, I'll never figure. Had I been as guilty of their misdeeds, I'd probably never sleep again. The world was indeed filled with a large assortment of puzzling people.

The rustle of Otsie's clothes against the dirt and rock sounded like the bawdy, rambunctious sounds of a saloon piano, but the Comancheros continued to sleep. Broken Nose had even stopped gargling so much, but it was the Papago I kept my eye on.

He lay on his side facing me, his angular forehead and protruding cheekbones buried in darkness. From time to time, the breeze fanned the coals, lighting his narrow chin.

Otsie reached the underbrush. To my ears, he sounded like a runaway stagecoach, but the Comancheros still slumbered. I forced myself to breathe slow and regular.

Slowly, I rose to a crouch, clutching a chunk of granite in either hand. I backed from the camp, feeling my way with my toes before stepping back.

Tulsa Jack rolled over and grunted.

Lutie moaned.

When I reached the underbrush, I turned and hurried into the loblollies after Otsie, hoping we wouldn't become separated this time.

Ahead, a small silhouette stood out against the backdrop of the moonlit clearing. I took his hand. "Let's go, boy." We broke into a trot up the mountainside through the loblollies. Ahead lay the talus slope, and the rattlesnakes.

Suddenly, gunshots erupted, shattering the silence of the night.

"They're gone."

"Why, you no-good . . ."

"It weren't my fault, Jack. I—"

"Shut up and get 'em, or I'll cowhide you all the way to Tucson."

Otsie looked up at me.

I knelt by him. "Now, look, boy. See that slope out there?"

"Yes, sir."

I pointed to the northwest. "You go straight up there. If you can't find the cave, you hide out during the day. There's plenty of spots to crawl into; just be sure you don't pick a hidey-hole that some rattler has already claimed.''

Behind us, the sound of pursuit drew closer.

His face was buried in darkness, but I heard the frown in his voice. ''But, Mr. Stonecipher. Aren't you going with me?''

A grin flickered across my face. ''I can't, boy. I've got to stop those jaspers. You've got to get back to the valley. You're the one we're all depending on.''

''But I want you to go with me.''

I grimaced. I didn't like the idea of turning him loose out there by himself, but there was no choice. ''I want to go, too, but I can't. *We* can't. We got to do what is before us. Now, you still remember what the entrance looks like, huh?''

Otsie nodded. ''I remember.''

''Okay.'' I turned him by his shoulders and pointed him up the slope of talus. ''Remember what to do if I don't get back.''

He nodded again.

''Now, git.'' I pushed him, and the boy took off in an all-out run. ''And watch for rattlers on the slope,'' I called softly.

By now, I could hear the footsteps of the Comancheros pounding over the pine needles. From the sound of their voices, they had spread into a skirmish line.

I remained by the edge of the clearing until Otsie was nothing but a dark shadow scrambling up the gray slope of shattered rock.

Finally, I turned back to the darkness of the loblolly forest, grabbing two more granite rocks to replace the ones I'd tossed away after escaping from the camp. I knelt, trying to pinpoint their positions.

I had to keep them from going after Otsie. He was now my only hope to save the women and children. But first, he had to elude the Comancheros, dodge the rattlesnakes, find the cave entrance, build the fire, and then tell my Apache brother the story—an almighty task for a six-year-old.

Tulsa Jack's gravelly voice came from off to my left. "The kid. Get the kid, Snag. He's heading for the gold."

Slipping to the edge of the forest to pick up light from the clearing, I moved back to my right, anticipating the Comanchero on that side to be the one taking up pursuit of Otsie.

A dark figure burst from behind a loblolly to my left. I spun and hurled a chunk of granite. At the same time, an explosion deafened me and a column of orange flame lit the air. Something grabbed at my shirt and yanked me around. In the next instant, a body fell on me, knocking me to the ground. I rolled and swung my fists, but the body was limp.

Without hesitation, I jumped to my feet and headed back to my right. Another shadow flew through the loblollies. I pulled up behind a thick bole and tossed the remaining chunk of granite beyond the approaching figure. The shadow jerked around at the noise the rock made when it bounced off a tree.

I leaped at the shadow, ducking my head and slamming my shoulder into the small of his back. Instead of going down, the shadow seemed to squirt forward and spin in midair, landing on his feet.

The Papago brought his rifle up, but I grabbed the muzzle and yanked, jerking him toward me. With his free hand, he grabbed for his knife, but I grasped his wrist and stepped under his oncoming body, spinning him over my back and slamming him to the forest floor.

I dropped on his chest, pinning his arms to the ground with my knees. I grabbed his knife and raised my arm, but for some reason, I hesitated.

Suddenly, the cold steel of a muzzle poked me in my ear.

"That's all she wrote, cowboy," Tulsa Jack grunted. "That's all she wrote."

I sat back, and the Papago squirmed from under me.

Tulsa Jack snarled, "I oughta blow your ornery head off, but I need you first." He jabbed me with the muzzle of his rifle. "Up."

I did as he said.

"Okay, Injun. Make yourself good for something. Tie 'im up good and proper. He gets away this time, and you'll take his place." He shook his head. "Blasted Injun. Worthless as a skunk."

His eyes blazing at Tulsa Jack, the Papago bound my wrists, twisting the rawhide deep into my flesh. I didn't pay too much attention to the pain in my wrists, for I was trying to pick out the shadows scooting across the slope of talus.

Jack saw me peering up the slope. He laughed, cold and cruel. "Don't count on nothing, cowboy. We'll bring that brat back. He can't get away from Snag. I'll teach him to run off again."

The remaining Comanchero wheezed to a halt by us. "Where's Snag?"

"After the kid," said Tulsa Jack. He yanked me around, then grabbed the Papago by his leather vest and yanked him nose-to-nose. "Now, git. Take this jasper back, you filthy Injun. And don't let 'im escape this time. You've caused us enough problems. Any Injun worth his salt could've saved us a heap of trouble. Now, git."

For a fleeting moment, the Papago and I locked eyes. He quickly looked away. "Go." He shoved me back down the slope. I stumbled, regained my footing, and then headed back to camp. A few minutes later, a terrifying shriek echoed across the mountainside. The Papago pulled up. He glanced up the mountain and grunted. ''That Snag, he ain't gonna catch him no boy tonight or no more.'' There was a faint chuckle in his voice.

His remarks reflected my own deduction upon hearing the scream. ''The boy got away,'' I observed without emotion, as if announcing that the sun had risen.

''Yes,'' replied the Papago, just as matter-of-factly.

Chapter Eleven

Lutie glowered at me when we entered the camp. "So, you're that rattlesnake man what made me shoot off my toe."

I said nothing.

The Papago gestured to a small boulder, and I plopped down in front of it. My ribs were sore as the dickens, but they weren't cracked. My hands began to tingle, a result of my wrists being bound too tightly.

Several minutes passed.

Lutie continued to stare at me, his black eyes glittering in the firelight. The Papago squatted, staring at me with indifference.

The first brilliant orange from the rising sun eased

over the horizon just as Tulsa Jack returned. Broken
Nose and the remaining Comanchero trailed behind.
Jack gave me a murderous look. "I oughta blow
your stinking head off."

"What happened, Jack?" Lutie looked up at the
big man, then cut his eyes toward Broken Nose and
frowned.

Tulsa Jack spat into the fire and glared at me. He
lay his hand on the butt of his revolver. "I
oughta . . ."

Broken Nose squatted and poured a cup of coffee.
"Snag's dead. Snakebit."

Lutie shook his head. "How?"

"He was after the kid, headin' full chisel up the
mountainside," said the remaining Comanchero.

I kept my eyes on Tulsa Jack. He had all the
earmarks of a boiler ready to explode.

Broken Nose continued, "He chased the kid up
that rocky slope. That's where he got bit. By the
time we got there, he was done dead. Snake got him
in the neck. He musta tripped and fell on the var-
mint."

Lutie wrinkled his nose and touched his dirt-
stained fingers to his neck. "Ugh." He changed the
subject. "What happened to you?"

Broken Nose glanced sheepishly at Lutie and
touched his nose. "I don't know. I was chasing the

kid. Next thing I knew, I was waking up. Reckon I run into a tree branch or something.''

Jack snorted. ''Sure, a tree branch. Tarnation, you blockhead. You didn't run into no tree branch.'' He nodded to me. ''This here jasper busted you with his Henry.'' Jack hooked his thumb toward my Brass Boy Henry they had brought in. ''Look at it. Still got blood on it.''

Broken Nose stared at Tulsa Jack, then he stared at me, trying to absorb what he had just been told. He pointed at me. ''You mean, this feller here, he swatted me with that rifle there?''

Jack laughed, a cold, sneering bray. ''What else, lummox? Yeah. He *swatted* you with the rifle barrel.''

Broken Nose's face twisted into a mask of anger. He grabbed for his six-gun. ''Why, you low-down, dirty—''

''Hold it,'' snapped Jack, grabbing the Comanchero's arm. ''You leave that hogleg in the holster. This hombre, no one ain't gonna plug him. He's got valuable information for us.''

Broken Nose yanked his arm away. ''But look what he did to me. And Snag. Snag's croaked, and it's this skunk's fault.''

''Yeah,'' Tulsa Jack hissed. ''You're right. It's all this here jasper's fault.'' He paused. A cruel grin played over his bearded face. His broad jaw looked like it had been carved from a block of granite. "I reckon he's gonna tell us what we want to hear. Besides, with Snag colder'n a wagon tire, we got his share to divvy up amongst us."

I spat at his feet. "Don't count on it, Jack. You're not gettin' a scrap of squat from me."

His face twisted into a ball of fury. "Why you . . ." He aimed a kick at my head.

I jerked aside, but his sharp-tined rowel caught the side of my face and opened a four-inch gash from chin to ear. Curses burst from my throat, and I twisted around on the ground and kicked at his feet.

My moccasin caught his ankle and knocked his foot from under him, sending him sprawling to the ground.

"What the . . ." He slammed to his back and kicked out at me with his boots.

I kicked back.

For several seconds, we lay there on our backs, cursing and kicking at each other with our feet. Suddenly, it dawned on Tulsa Jack that he could get to his feet, so he rolled away, jumped up, and yanked out his six-gun.

He jammed it against my forehead and cocked the trigger. "You're dead, you—"

"Hold on, Jack," said Broken Nose. "You kill him, and we don't get the gold."

Tulsa Jack's face burned crimson red. The veins in the side of his neck bulged with suppressed anger. His finger whitened as he squeezed on the trigger. "I don't give a . . ."

"He's right, Jack," Lutie added. "Think about the gold."

Jack hesitated. Blood flowed back into his finger. Reluctantly, he pulled the muzzle from my forehead. "I'm still gonna kill this jasper. You wait and see."

By now, the sun had risen above the horizon and bathed the camp with its early-morning warmth.

"Yeah," muttered Tulsa Jack. "I reckon you boys is right, but I don't see no sense in waiting to find out where the gold is, do you?" He gave me a cruel sneer and reached for his knife.

A cold chill raced through my body. I knew exactly what he meant.

"Well, cowboy. You ready to tell us where that gold come from?" He held the knife blade up and ran his thumb over the cutting edge. "Huh?"

"Forget it, Jack."

His sneer broadened. "I'm kinda glad you said that. I'd hate to let you off easy with a slug between the eyes." He held the Arkansas toothpick and caught glimmers of sunlight from it. "I'm going to enjoy making you talk."

I spat at him.

His faced darkened, and he nodded to Broken Nose. "String him up to that there pine. I reckon he'll start spilling his guts after I peel a few strips of skin from his back."

Lutie hobbled to his feet and sneered at me while Broken Nose slashed the rawhide around my wrists. "Stick them hands in front."

I brought my hands in front of my body and crossed my wrists. While Lutie and Tulsa Jack looked on, Broken Nose looped a strip of rawhide around my hands. I yanked back, jerking him forward, then with a mighty heave, shoved him back into his three cohorts, sending all four sprawling to the ground.

Instantly, I spun and headed for the underbrush, but a booming explosion and the smack of lead against the boulder at my side stopped me in my tracks. I hesitated, then put my hands up immediately. "All right, all right. I'm not going nowhere."

I clenched my teeth and cursed myself for stopping. Another two steps, and I'd been in the underbrush. I might've made it. Just didn't have guts enough to take the chance.

Broken Nose tied my wrists like he was hog-tying a wild longhorn. At the same time, the other Comanchero tossed a lariat over an overhanging limb, and Broken Nose lashed the end around my bonds.

They stretched my arms high, lifting my feet so

that only my toes touched the ground. My extended muscles screamed.

The Comancheros leered at me. The Papago stared impassively. I locked eyes with him. For a brief moment, I saw a flicker of life in his, but it died instantly.

Tulsa Jack hawked on his knife and rubbed the spittle along the cutting edge with his thumb. "Yeah. I'm going to enjoy this."

I didn't figure I had the chance of a wad of spit in a dust storm, but as Jack approached, I swung back on the rope and slammed my feet into his chest, sending him tumbling backward, head over heels.

Broken Nose and the second Comanchero rushed me. I got off a quick kick, managing to slam my heel into Broken Nose's swollen face.

He screamed piteously and grabbed his nose. Blood spurted from beneath his hands. The second Comanchero wrapped his arms around my legs. I struggled, but to no avail.

"That did it!" Tulsa Jack shouted. "I'm gonna cut you to pieces. To blazes with the gold. Ain't no jasper alive gonna do to me what you done and get away with it."

He raised the knife over his head. "I'm gonna cut your stinking head clean off."

Suddenly, a frail, feminine voice cut through the

silence between shouts. "Help, please, help me! Help me."

Well, we all froze, Jack with the knife in mid-swing. The Comanchero who held my legs dropped them and turned to the voice. Broken Nose blinked away the tears in his eyes, and the Papago stared hard at me.

Grace Miller staggered from the underbrush, one hand holding her shawl about her shoulders, the other reaching out to the Comancheros. "Please, help me, help me!"

She sank to the ground while the Comancheros just stared at her, dumbfounded.

With a dramatic sigh, she rolled onto her back and closed her eyes.

Tulsa Jack pointed to Broken Nose. "See what she wants."

He shook his head. "My nose hurts too bad, Jack. That jasper kicked on it again." He shook his head. "It sure hurts."

Jack gestured to the remaining Comanchero. "You see to her."

"I'll see to her!" shouted Lutie eagerly, hobbling on one foot toward the supine woman.

"Forget it," Tulsa Jack snarled. "I don't want you around her. I'll see what's wrong with her."

Lutie jerked to a halt, looking around at Jack with an injured expression on his face. "Aw, Jack."

"I mean it. You back away. I'll see to the woman."

Tulsa Jack knelt beside Grace. "What's wrong with you, woman?" His gravelly voice quivered with cruel anticipation.

Grace moaned, and her hand dropped away from her shawl.

Jack froze. "Huh?" His eyes rolled down to gaze upon his belly, which had the muzzle of a Colt .44 poked two inches in it.

Grace said, "You tell those filthy animals of yours to drop their guns or I'll kill you. Pure and simple. On the count of three."

The sharp click of a drawn hammer echoed through the silence of the camp. "One . . . two . . . th—"

"Hold it, hold it!" Jack threw up his hands. "Hold it."

Before any of the Comancheros could react, Dora Barton stepped from the underbrush, the other six-gun in her hand. "We'll shoot," she said simply.

The Comancheros jerked around. From either side, John Edward, Marline Ray, and Otsie appeared, holding crude spears in their hands. "Do what Mama says," said John Edward.

"Yeah," put in Otsie.

"Drop the guns," Grace ordered.

"Do what she says, boys," Tulsa Jack replied.

Five minutes later, I was free and the Comancheros were tied tighter than a twisted fritter.

Afterward, we all hugged and bragged, all the while grinning like possums in a hen house. "That was the bravest thing I ever saw, Mrs. Barton," I said. "For everyone," I added.

"Well, I must admit," she replied sheepishly, "I was afraid, but John Edward and Marline Ray were so brave, I shamed myself."

I grinned at all of them. "I'm proud of all of you."

Otsie tugged on my arm. "What do we do now, Mr. Stonecipher?"

"Well, boy." I studied the surly Comancheros. "They got horses. I reckon we'll take their animals and head out for Tucson." I grinned at Tulsa Jack. "You don't mind, do you, Jack? If you think you'd get lonesome here, I'll send up some smoke to bring you company."

He shook his head adamantly. "No. No. We ain't gonna get lonesome. You just go ahead and take the horses. Don't send up no smoke, you hear? We'll be just fine here. Honest."

I shook my head. "I don't know." I winked at Grace. "I sure hate to leave them out here all by themselves. No telling what could happen."

She grimaced. "It would be terrible."

"No. No, don't worry about us," Jack begged. "Don't worry nothing at all about us. We don't need no company."

We were all feeling pretty smug. Here we were, me, two women, and three children, and we'd hog-tied a band of vicious Comancheros. Not a bad job. Not a bad day's work.

Nature always seemed to find a way to keep everything in balance. We must've been too smug, for in the next few seconds, everything changed for us.

"Look, Mr. Stonecipher," said Otsie, pointing out across the desert to the east. "What's that dust?"

My blood ran cold.

Tulsa Jack sneered. "Now what, *Mr. Stonecipher*?"

Grace frowned up at me. "What's wrong, Andy?"

I was speechless.

Dora Barton started. "What does he mean, Mr. Stonecipher? What's wrong?"

"Tell 'em, Mr. Stonecipher!" shouted Tulsa Jack in his gruff, guttural voice. "Tell 'em what's wrong."

"Shut up." I glared at the sneering grin on his face. I wanted to knock it off, but he was tied. That was the difference between him and me. "One of these days, Jack, it's gonna be just you and me. And I'm going to almighty enjoy that day."

He laughed again.

Alarmed, Grace jerked on my arm. "Andy. What's going on? Tell us. What's happening?"

I pointed to the dust. "See that? It's more of his boys."

For a moment, they studied the situation.

"We've got guns. Let's fight them off."

"It isn't that easy. Yeah, we've got guns, but they have us outnumbered, and sooner or later, they'd get us."

Dora Barton wrung her hands. "What do we do?"

"All right." I took a deep breath. "Here's what we do. First, we blindfold these jaspers. We don't want them to see where we're going. Then, we'll take all their guns and cartridges."

"What about the horses?" John Edward asked.

"I wish we could. We can't."

"But they'll fit," he replied.

I winced. "Quiet. I said, no. The horses stay. We'll take the guns. That'll give us enough fire-power." I paused and looked at each of them. "Okay?"

They nodded.

"All right. Grace, you blindfold them. I'll load

thc others down with guns and then come back and help. And make the blindfolds tight. We don't want them to know where we're heading.''

She nodded.

While I was loading the children with guns, I whispered to John Edward. ''Go that direction.'' I pointed to the northeast.

He whispered back. ''That's not the right way.''

''I know.'' I hooked my thumb over my shoulder toward the Comancheros. ''They'll see you head out that way. Then when they're blindfolded, we'll cut back.''

He grinned. ''Okay. I understand.''

I glanced out across the desert. The oncoming riders were about an hour away. We had to hurry.

''I'll blindfold the Papago,'' I said.

The Indian glared at me, and I'll swear, a faint grin touched the edge of his lip for a fleeting second.

Chapter Twelve

The morning sun blistered us as we stumbled and staggered across the slope of talus. I slipped my arm around Mrs. Barton's waist. She jerked away. "Just what do you think you're doing, Mr. Stonecipher?" Her face contorted in shock.

"Just wanted to help, ma'am," I said, quickly backing away and stumbling as I did so. "I just figured you might need some help getting across this rocky slope."

She sniffed. "I didn't need any help getting down the mountain earlier."

I glanced at Grace, who grinned sheepishly. "She's right, Andy. She managed just fine."

"See." Mrs. Barton tossed her head and continued up the slope. After three steps, she stumbled, but quickly caught herself and continued upward, never looking back.

The riders in the desert were about thirty minutes out. I looked up the mountain. The cloud-scraping loblollies would hide us as we clambered up the last leg to the hidden passage.

When we reached the top of the talus slope, I sent the others ahead, cautioning them once again of the trip rope at the exit of the passage.

"What are you going to do?" Worry knitted Grace's forehead.

"Stay and watch." I gestured to the camp with my Brass Boy. "I don't know if we fooled them or not. One of those jaspers could have wiggled his way loose and got a look at us."

"Can I stay?" Otsie stepped forward.

"Me, too," said John Edward. "I can help."

I couldn't have been prouder of the two if they'd been my own sprouts. I winked at them. "This is a one-man job, boys. You take your the women back to the valley. Get things situated. Check the traps. Get what fish we got, and make sure the water jug's full. We might need it."

Without argument, they nodded and turned back to the cave.

Grace hesitated. She looked at me, her face pale and drawn.

I grinned. "I'll be along. Just you all get going."

As I watched them disappear back into the passage, strange feelings rumbled through my body, feelings I couldn't explain. Once, I would have been tickled to be shed of any obligations or entanglements with other folk, but something about these families, even Mrs. Barton and Marline Ray, was different, like—I don't know. I couldn't find the right word. It was just a different feeling, that's all I can say.

Down below, the riders reached the foothills. I grimaced. There were six of them. Counting the Papago, Tulsa Jack now had nine men, ten including himself.

Keeping the loblollies between me and the camp, I eased back down the slope. If they spotted me, I could turn back into the foothills, but I didn't plan on any of them, not even the Papago, laying an eye on me. I kept my fingers crossed. Once they headed off on the false trail we'd laid, I'd rest easier.

For the next thirty minutes, there was no movement in the vicinity of the camp even though it was hidden behind the loblollies and underbrush. Still, I would have seen any Comanchero riding onto the rocky slopes above the loblollies.

As I watched, all ten Comancheros stepped from

the underbrush three hundred yards distant. One emerged from the gang and pointed up the slope in the direction of the hidden passage.

I blinked, rubbed my balled fists into my eyes, and then looked again. He was still pointing. Who in the blazes was that hombre? I tried to pick out his features, but all I could tell was that he was lean as a winter-gaunted bear and brown as sun-baked leather.

A heavy weight sagged down on my shoulders. I felt like I didn't have a breath left. *Blast!* They'd found someone who knew of the hidden valley. I took a deep breath. After several deliberate seconds, I jerked the Brass Boy to my shoulder. I had no choice now.

But I hesitated, a tiny voice in the back of my mind nagging at me, wondering if that owlhoot could have just been pointing at a hawk or—or at anything. But I knew better. There was no hawk around, no reason for him to be pointing up there except that he knew the location of the hidden passage.

The gang of ten started up the slope.

"Well, tarnation and back, Andy," I muttered to myself as I positioned myself on one knee and braced the Brass Boy against a loblolly. "It appears you got your work cut out for you, boy. So, might as well get to it."

I adjusted the ladder sights and centered the front sights of the Brass Boy on the jasper in the lead, the one who had pointed out the passage. I didn't like killing, but there were two women and three children up there who would end up in the dregs of Mexico if I didn't do something.

I calculated the distance between me and the Comancheros at around three hundred yards. The Henry slug, two hundred and sixteen grains of lead powered by forty of black powder, was a powerful-hitting cartridge. But the slug dropped fast, about eight inches in a hundred yards, so I held the sliver of a front sight about two feet above the jasper's chest.

At such a distance, I couldn't plan the shot. All I could hope was to hit the hombre—at least, knock him out of the fray.

I tightened my finger, then backed away, hoping the Comancheros would change directions, but they continued northwest up the slope. Taking a deep breath, I released part of it, then took up slack on the trigger again. Gently, I continued pressing, not jerking, but gently pressing harder and harder.

The Henry and I had been together for years, and I knew exactly when the .44-caliber rifle would fire. And, at that instant, it fired.

Down below, the gang of Comancheros jerked around just as the owlhoot in front caught the slug and hurtled backward, sprawling across the rocky clearing like a rag doll. In the next instant, the other nine vanished back into the underbrush.

I hated to waste ammunition, for the remaining thirteen slugs were all I had for the Henry, but then, I'd sent four Winchesters and probably two hundred rounds back with the others. More than enough.

I peered across the slope. *After all,* I told myself, *nine-to-one odds isn't any too attractive.* Maybe by chance, I could lower them. Immediately, I sprayed the underbrush into which they had ducked. The mountainside reverberated with the echo of thirteen explosions.

I got lucky. One Comanchero screamed and fell from the underbrush into the clearing. He lay motionless. I didn't put another slug into him. Even if I'd had any, I wouldn't. If he wasn't dead, he was badly hurt. Like Lutie, the nine-toed Comanchero, this hombre wasn't going to cause us any trouble.

In the next second, the entire mountainside erupted with gunfire. Slugs hummed all around me. I pressed up against the loblolly, grateful for its bulky bole.

But I knew I had no time to waste.

While they were potshotting me, they were also moving up to surround me. I had to move, and move now, despite the gunfire. I just hoped that none of them had a Sharps Buffalo rifle. At three hundred yards, a Winchester or Henry wasn't much better than a bow and arrow, but a Sharps—well, that was another matter entirely.

Dropping into a crouch, I darted across the clearing, edging toward the underbrush. I didn't dare cut up across the slope of talus. If they followed me across the ridges, I could lead them astray.

But they didn't follow.

Instead, they continued northwest up the slope.

I cursed myself. In a burst of idiotic emotion, I'd emptied my Henry and sure accomplished a lot. Why, other than that one jasper in the underbrush, I reckoned I probably killed or injured two dozen twigs.

And now, when I needed a straight-shooting rifle to deter them, I had no cartridges. I'd used them all killing twigs. "You stupid, bullheaded idiot," I muttered vehemently. "You better figure out something. And fast."

I didn't have a choice. There was no choice.

Breaking into a run, I raced south, hoping to vanish into the distant foothills. I figured on dropping below one of the ridges and slipping back up to the rimrock. Once on top, I'd make my way to the valley and shinny down the narrow chimney I had climbed earlier. *Maybe,* I told myself desperately, *maybe if I can reach the rimrock, I can keep them out with a landslide.*

The rocky ground slashed at my moccasins. I clenched my teeth as slivery shards of granite punched holes in the soles. I couldn't take time to repack the moccasins.

After topping the first ridge, I cut back up the mountain, darting through the loblollies. Back to my right, half a mile north, the band of Comancheros stumbled their way ever closer to the hidden passage.

The slope ahead of me sheared upward precipitously. With a groan of anguish, I leaped forward, grasping at the sharp granite with my fingers as I clambered upward, scrambling frantically for the rimrock. I dug my toes into the razor edges of protruding granite, feeling nothing but the hopelessness that comes from desperation.

"No. No," I muttered between clenched teeth as I scaled the towering ramparts of the Baboquivaris, hoping to head off the Comancheros.

Finally, I crawled onto the rimrock and stood, gasping for breath. My chest heaved, and my lungs burned, a bitter, caustic sensation that raced up my throat, stripping it so raw I couldn't swallow.

I choked and leaned forward, resting my hands on my knees. I gasped for breath. There was no time to waste. I threw my head back and sucked in several deep breaths, then broke into a run toward the hidden entrance. My bloody feet pounded across the rocky plateau. "Please," I whispered. "Please, let me get there first."

They beat me.

When I drew up on the rimrock above the hidden entrance, the band of Comancheros was standing in front of the entrance, deep in discussion. Tulsa Jack gesticulated wildly at the Papago, but the Indian slowly shook his head.

I wanted to shout, to scream my frustration. Instead, ignoring any essence of cool and calm reasoning, I kicked and threw rocks down on them.

They scattered, shouting and cursing, following that up with several gunshots aimed in my direction.

For me, the burst of anger was an exercise in futility, doing no good, accomplishing nothing except to reaffirm in their sodden brains that indeed this was the entrance they sought.

With a groan, I banged the heel of my hand against my forehead—several times. For all I knew, they might have dismissed that cave. Probably not, but maybe. Now we'd never know, for in my infinite wisdom, I'd pointed out exactly the cave I didn't want them to find.

"Smart, Andy," I muttered. "Smart."

Down below, the shouting died away. I heard footsteps scrambling over the rocks, so I tossed a few more boulders down.

The shouts and gunfire started again.

But I knew I couldn't keep this up. Rocks against slugs? Forget it.

I turned back to the valley. I had to get down to the women and children. I figured I could reach them before the Comancheros as I clambered down the chimney, paying no attention to my bloody moccasins or the slashes on my hands. Besides, we had traps set. That would slow the outlaws.

The narrow chimney didn't seem to have as many footholds as I remembered, for I fell more than I climbed down. When I reached the bottom, I looked at the cave exit. The rocks still perched above. An unbidden chuckle escaped my lips. Someone, one of the Comancheros, was sure in for a surprise.

A shout from behind jerked me around.

Otsie and John Edward came running. "We saw you coming down!" shouted the older boy. "What's wrong?"

I glared at them, ignoring his question. "Where's your guns?"

They froze, glanced at each other, then looked up sheepishly at me.

I waved them back to the cave. "Get up there. Get some guns. We're going to need them. Now! We got maybe five minutes."

They scurried up to the cave with me right behind them. In just a few minutes, we were going to have a host of unwelcome guests in our valley, and we had to set up a proper greeting for them.

To my surprise, we did just that.

No one panicked. No one squalled. No one called out for Mama. They all listened to what I said, and then set out to carry out their orders.

We had four Winchesters and six Colts. Mrs. Barton and Grace took Winchesters. I gave each boy a Winchester, then handed Marline Ray a Colt from which I had secretly removed the cartridges, and I loaded myself down with the remaining five Colts.

Me and the boys hurried back down into the valley. The women and Marline Ray remained on the ledge above, a deadly position to catch the Comancheros in a crossfire, even if the trap was made up of two women and three children.

I figured seven, maybe eight outlaws were coming for us.

A war stared us in the face, and we were blamed well going to meet it. I set the boys in positions near the trail. "Now when they get here, they got the rock slide to tolerate, then the traps along the trail. With luck, maybe that'll take care of two or three. Don't start shooting until they get past the last trap, but boys . . ."

I paused, looked each in the eye, square and honest. "Boys, this ain't for fun. They'll hurt you and your ma bad. Marline Ray, too, John Edward. So, when you spot them, shoot.''

John Edward blinked. ''You mean . . . you mean, shoot like to . . . to hurt them?''

How do you tell a boy the truth about life? Just open and honest, I guess. So that's what I did. ''Not to hurt, boy. Shoot to kill. If you don't, he'll hurt you bad.''

Otsie looked up at me. ''Mr. Stonecipher.''

''Yeah, boy.'' I glanced around, watching the mouth of the passage while waiting for him to speak. ''What is it?''

''Mr. Stonecipher, I . . . I'm scared. I-I don't know if I can shoot them.''

I looked back at the boys. Their faces were pale, their eyes bugged out. John Edward's Adam's apple bobbed like a perch cork. I cursed those Comancheros for making these boys have to face such a despicable truth so young in their lives.

''Sorry, boy.'' I laid my hand on his shoulder. ''We got no choice. Those hombres, they're coming in here for you and your family. You can't let 'em take you. It ain't a simple thing to figure out, but from what I've seen of you two younkers, you're men enough to do what you got to do.''

John Edward nodded. ''I . . . I think I can, Mr. Stonecipher. I think I can.''

Otsie looked up at the older boy, then turned to me. "Me, too. I think I can."

I shook my head. These boys should've been back East, out of this kind of trouble, but they weren't, so they had to face it.

"Okay. You know where you need to be. Get there. And remember—they start getting too close to you, hightail it back up the trail to the cave. You hear? And don't stop for nothing."

They nodded, too choked with fear to speak. Quickly, they hid behind boulders.

I felt the same way. I pulled a Colt and cocked the hammer. "Okay, Tulsa Jack. You boys come on out," I muttered as I hid behind a loblolly at the end of the trail. "Let's strike up the fiddle."

Chapter Thirteen

Overhead, a mockingbird fussed. At the far end of the valley, a hawk screeched, and behind me, a trout broke the icy waters of the bottomless lake. The sun felt warm and lazy on my shoulders, and the morning air smelled of fresh grass and clover. It was a morning to relax and enjoy nature, not to kill.

I glanced at the mouth of the cave, at the wedge of rocks and boulders stacked above the entrance. Then I followed the trail from the entrance down to us, pausing to study each sapling tied back in a sharp arch. On two or three of the slender trees, we had fastened sharpened sticks. As I crouched, waiting for Tulsa Jack and his Comancheros, I cursed

myself for not lashing sharp stakes to all of the saplings.

I looked back at the hidden passage. Nothing.

I blinked, and, as if by magic, there the Comancheros stood, just inside the cave, peering out
across the valley. For several seconds, they remained motionless, staring into the hidden canyon.

Crouching lower behind the loblolly, I waited.
From where I hid, I could see the boys. They spotted the outlaws and looked at me.

I nodded. "Easy," I whispered, knowing full
well they couldn't hear me. "Not too soon. Not too
soon. Let the traps do their job first."

A moment later, the owlhoots stepped from the
cave. One stumbled, then looked down. He pointed
at the ground and yelled, but his words were smothered by the thunder of rocks and boulders tumbling
down on them.

As one, the group froze, measuring the distance
back to the cave, then screaming, turned back down
the trail as the first rocks hurtled among them.

The first Comanchero hit the trail at full chisel,
and the first limb smacked him squarely across the
forehead, knocking him unconscious to the rocky
ground. The others ignored him, leaping over his
limp body as they flushed like a covey of quail in
an effort to escape the landslide.

The sprung traps made a *swupping* sound as they

whipped forward, and for the next few seconds, the air was filled with shouts, screams, and *swups*. There came a *swup* and a scream, a *swup* and a shout, a *swup* and a curse.

Finally, the first of the Comancheros emerged from the trail, and we met them with blistering gunfire, which added to their confusion. Several ducked back up the trail, only to collide with those trying to escape the traps.

I don't know if the boys hit anyone, but I do know that they chopped up the countryside. Slugs whizzed past, a couple gouging out chunks from the loblolly behind which I crouched. I stayed low.

Picking my targets carefully, I fired, but between the limbs springing back and forth, Comancheros darting about like possum-chased chickens, and slugs doing a square dance on the woods around me, I couldn't tell if I hit anyone or not, but I emptied five six-guns in less than a couple of minutes.

As quickly as it had begun, the fight was over, at least for the time being. The Comancheros disappeared back into the cave, leaving two of their own sprawled on the rocky trail.

Otsie and John Edward looked around at me. They started to stand, but I waved them down. John Edward didn't understand. He stood and held his cupped hand to his ear.

Before I could shout, a shot rang out from inside

the passage and smashed into the boulder not six inches from John Edward's head. He understood that. He dropped to his knees fast.

I motioned for them to remain where they were. Quickly, I reloaded the six-guns and studied the cave. There were still six in there. Too bad one of those on the trail wasn't Tulsa Jack, I told myself, letting my eyes play back over the inert bodies.

Then the gunfire ceased.

No one moved. We remained behind our boulders and trees, the Comancheros in the cave. An hour passed, then another. The sun grew hotter.

I poked my head from behind the loblolly and peered at the black mouth of the cave. Were they still inside?

A fraction of a second after I pulled my head back, a slug tore up a chunk of ground the size of my fist right where my head had been. For a moment, I stared at the hole, confused. There was no way a slug from the cave could have struck in that spot.

Then I realized where it had come from. I looked up, and my blood ran cold.

Two dark figures stood on the rim of the canyon, looking down upon us. I muttered a curse. They had us, like the proverbial fish in a barrel. They fired again, this time at the boys.

Otsie and John Edward crouched behind their boulders.

There was no time to waste. The boys were out among the rocks and boulders, much easier targets than me back in the loblollies. We couldn't reach the trail to the cave. We'd be swatted down as easily as stomping ants. The only chance we had was back in the loblollies until dark.

I didn't take time to yell. I pulled two Colts and started firing at the figures above. "Come on, boys!" I shouted. "Move them feet and get over here."

Slug after slug I pumped at the figures above, who dropped to their knees out of harm's way.

The boys hesitated. "Now. I mean now." I only had a few slugs left in the two six-guns.

Like frightened rabbits, they exploded from behind the boulders and zigzagged down the rocky slope to the loblollies. Shots boomed from the cave, but whistled harmlessly over the boys' heads. It was the two jaspers on the rimrock who had the angle, and I had to keep them pinned down until the boys reached me.

Seconds later, the boys dashed into the loblollies and crouched behind the thick-boled pines.

In the next instant, the gunfire from above continued, but we relaxed. As long as we remained within the copse of pines, we were safe, unless a ricocheting slug found one of us.

As the afternoon drew on, the Comancheros above grew weary of shooting into the pines. Finally, they ceased altogether, but I could see their heads peering over the rim, watching, patiently waiting for a mistake on our part.

The other owlhoots remained in the cave, none daring to venture out.

A standoff. One side waiting for the other to make a move.

I glanced toward the cave with the women. From time to time, one appeared in the mouth, but neither made an attempt to communicate or come down. A grin curled my lips. They were learning. Too bad that kind of learning had to return to the East.

"Okay, boys," I said as the sun disappeared over the rim of the canyon. "Stay where you are, but listen. Soon as it's dark enough, we'll slip up to the cave. Come morning, they'll have us if we stay down here. So when I tell you, you move out. Take the trail to the cave, and try to be as quiet as you can. You hear?"

"Yes, sir."

"Yes, sir. Ah, Mr. Stonecipher?" John Edward's voice was strained with fear.

"Yeah, boy?"

"Ah, once we reach the cave. What then? Won't
... won't they have us trapped?"

I didn't have time to explain. "Trust me on this,
boy. There's no time now to talk about it."

A flurry of gunfire ended our discussion. Slugs
ripped through the pines, sent needles tumbling
through the air, splattered chunks of bark across the
ground.

A pinecone dropped nearby. I ignored it.

Another flurry of gunshots splattered the pines,
and moments later, another pinecone fell. I
shrugged it off. With all the slugs tearing up the
pines, falling pinecones meant nothing—but a
strange feeling raised the hair on the back of my
neck. I pressed closer against the thick bole of the
pine.

A heavy silence dropped over the valley.

I sat, and waited.

Within seconds, a single shot rang out, followed
moments later by a pinecone bouncing off my
shoulder. I scooted back and peered around the side
of the loblolly.

The Papago stood on the rim, and as I watched,
he fired again and ducked back behind a boulder.
This time, I heard the slug strike the top of the pine
and moments later, here came another pinecone
bouncing down through the limbs and dropping not
five feet from where I crouched.

Despite our situation, I couldn't suppress a faint grin at the Indian's taunting. Unable to find us in his sights, he resorted to the next best thing, chucking pinecones at us.

"Well, partner," I whispered, bringing my Colt up, "two can play that game." I waited.

In the next breath, he reappeared and fired. I shot back at the same time, deliberately trying to hit the large boulder behind which he hid.

The slug splattered not five feet from the Papago. He jumped back and stumbled out of sight. I settled back and chuckled, remembering the old saw my grandfather taught me: "Don't give folks nothing you wouldn't want them to give back."

I laughed again. That made sense to me.

Night came early down in the canyon, gathering dark shadows and pouring them across the valley floor like black paint. Silently, I gathered the boys while some light remained.

A few minutes later, we pushed out. "Now, stay close to me. We move quiet, they'll never spot us."

Otsie spoke in a frail voice. "Mr. Stonecipher, I can't see nothing anyway. I can't even see you."

"Don't worry. You won't get lost. Give me your hand, and John Edward, you take his other hand. We'll go slow." We fumbled for each other's hands.

"Can't we wait until the moon is up? We can see where we're going that way."

"And they can see us."

"Oh."

"Grab hold, and let's go."

Shucking my revolver, I eased through the pines slowly, feeling our way with my six-gun. Once we left the pines, the darkness would not be so complete.

The boys held tight and didn't utter a word. I was proud of them.

Carefully, we made our way out of the pines and into the rocks. From the rocks under my feet, I picked the trail, staying with the rocks worn smooth over years of use. Gradually, my night vision improved, and I could make out the vague white glow at our feet.

Suddenly, a great ball of flames dropped from the sky, lighting the rocky slope on which we stood. I looked up in time to see another ball of flame roll over the rim of the canyon and plunge to the slope below.

"There they are," a voice shouted.

Gunfire erupted from the hidden passage.

I returned fire, at the same time shouting at the boys, "Run! The trail! Hurry."

They darted past me, and I followed, throwing off wild shots.

Slugs tore up the ground and bounced off the rocks around us. John Edward reached the trail and raced upward.

From the hidden passage came shouts. I guessed the Comancheros were after us, but they faced the disadvantage we faced—the darkness. And the flickering shadows cast by the fire were deceiving.

I ran crouched over as I ascended the trail, hoping to make a smaller target. Slugs ricocheting off the canyon wall could do a heap of damage.

"There they go. Up that trail."

"Now we got 'em!" shouted a guttural voice.

"You bet, Jack," I muttered.

It was an eerie sight, the canyon lit by the reddish glow of flames, punctuated by bright-orange bursts of gunfire.

We reached the log and crossed quickly, after which we dumped it down the chasm and hurried into the cave where the others waited. Wisely, they had extinguished the small fire.

"What was that?" a voice from below shouted as the noise of the falling log died away.

"Who cares? Hurry. Get 'em."

"I'm almost—Yaaaaaaaa!"

We jerked around at the scream.

Grace whispered. "What was that?"

"We moved the log."

I didn't have to explain further. They were down to six.

"Oh."

"What now, Mr. Stonecipher?" Mrs. Barton's voice was low, but I could hear the fear in it.

"We wait, Mrs. Barton. They can't reach us without the log, and it's a hundred feet below."

The moon rose in the east, lighting the hidden valley with a cold blue light.

Tulsa Jack's voice carried through the night. "Lutie! You still up there?"

A voice echoed from the canyon rim. "Yeah, Jack. Me and the Injun."

"You got your lariat?"

"Yeah."

"Well, then. Drop one end. Tie the other up there. We'll swing across the break in the trail."

Grace gasped.

My first thought was to shoot each one as he landed on our side, but Jack's next order knocked me back on my heels. "The rest of you, shoot any hombre who comes out of that cave over there. I don't want no one jumping out and taking a potshot at me while I'm swinging on a rope."

I couldn't take on six, especially when two were straight above me, so I knelt by the fire and stirred the coals. A small flame sprang to life.

Hastily, I shaved the head of two dry creosote branches to make torches.

"Now listen. This cave behind us leads out, but it twists and turns, so we've got to stay together."

I expected someone to insist on remaining behind, unwilling to take the chance, but I was wrong. No one, not even Marline Ray, argued. After sticking a couple of more creosote branches under my belt, I led the way back into the cave, giving Grace the second torch to bring up the rear.

For several yards the cave twisted and turned, then began descending. The walls grew colder, and the musty smell of damp soil clogged my nostrils.

"Hold it." I stopped abruptly.

"What's wrong?"

"Ahead, there's a hole in the floor. Move over next to the wall. There's plenty of room to pass."

"A hole?" Otsie whispered. "How big?"

"Shush," his mother said.

Carefully, we made our way around the gaping chasm, then continued down the cave.

"How . . . how long is this cave?" Grace asked.

"I-I don't know for sure."

Mrs. Barton spoke up. "Don't you remember?"

"No." I continued pushing ahead. "I've never been down here."

"You've *what?*" Mrs. Barton choked.

I looked around, holding the torch out so we

could see one another. "I said I've never been down here, but my Apache father told me of it. He said it opens into another valley, and if he said that, then it does."

"Mama, I'm scared," whined Marline Ray.

Mrs. Barton hesitated, then whispered, "Hush, child. Everything's going to be fine . . . Mr. Stonecipher, he knows what he's doing."

My first torch burned down, so I lit a second, and one for Grace also. If we were going to find a way out, we had to do it quickly. The cave continued to descend.

Thirty minutes later, only six inches remained of my second torch. We had passed two more chasms, but had seen no evidence of anyone having been down here before us. Could Horse of Water have been mistaken?

"Andy?" Grace's voice was frail and thin.

"Yeah?"

"My torch is almost gone."

I gulped. We had to keep going. I didn't mind feeling my way through the darkness, but those gaping chasms in the floor of the cave gave a whole different slant to the idea.

Otsie's tiny voice came from the dark. "What are we going to do when we run out of light, Mr. Stonecipher?"

"He's just going to keep going, ain't that right, Mr. Stonecipher?" said John Edward.

Mrs. Barton retorted. "Don't say ain't, John Edward."

"Oh, Ma."

"You heard me, young man."

John Edward groaned. "Yes, ma'am."

My torch flickered. I caught my breath.

Ahead, the cave made a turn to the right. As I rounded the bend, a grin leaped to my face. Stuck in a fissure in the wall were four large torches. "Look!" I shouted. "Look."

You'd thought we'd discovered a pot of gold, but then gold isn't the same to all people. To us, the torches were worth more than all the pots of gold in the world.

I grabbed a torch and touched the last flame of my small torch to it. A bright flame leaped up, and the new firebrand lit the entire cave.

A wave of relief washed over me. I grinned at the others. "Let's go." I had no idea where we were, but I tried to bolster their spirits with a white lie. "We should be almost there." Before we continued, I handed Grace an unlit torch. "Just in case," I added.

She nodded. "I understand."

The cave took a broad curve to the left, then a sharp right. We rounded the last bend and halted.

Mrs. Barton screamed. Marline Ray started crying. Grace caught her breath.

The floor of the cave had turned to water.

Chapter Fourteen

I studied the cave ahead, but the longer I stood staring, the more frustrated I became. We didn't have a choice. We couldn't go back. "Now listen," I said, turning to face the others. "I'm going ahead, to see what's out there. You wait here."

Mrs. Barton and Marline Ray had their arms wrapped about each other, their eyes threatening tears. Grace whispered, "Be careful."

"Don't worry," I replied in an effort to be light-hearted. "I can't swim too good."

But no one laughed.

Taking a deep breath, I waded into the water. To my surprise, it remained ankle-deep to the next bend, some twenty feet. I waved them forward. "It's okay."

Gingerly, they eased into the water. Mrs. Barton gasped, and Marline Ray sobbed.

John Edward hissed. "Hush up, crybaby."

As they drew near, I continued down the cave. Slowly, the water rose.

"It's getting deeper, Andy." Grace's voice was tight with strain.

A sense of gloom settled over us, pressing closer even than the black water.

"We're still doing all right," I replied, trying to keep their spirits up. "Just keep going."

"Well, I sure ain't going back," said Otsie.

I chuckled. "I don't think any of us want to do that, boy."

Grace laughed, and even Marline Ray giggled. The mood lightened even though the water grew deeper.

Time came to a standstill in the cave.

But we trudged forward, pushing into the black water ahead of us. My legs ached, and I could imagine how the women and children must have felt. Soon, we were going to have to stop and rest, not that we could gain much relief standing waist-deep in cold water.

Suddenly, my feet dropped out from under me, and I plunged beneath the surface of the icy water. Instinctively, I held the torch high and kicked my feet frantically, driving me back to the surface.

I came up sputtering and coughing.

"Andy, Andy!"

"Stay back." I coughed and spit out water. "There's a drop-off." A terrifying fear plunged through my heart. I had stepped into one of the bottomless chasms. A crazy idea flashed into my brain. What if a whirlpool suddenly developed, sucking us all deep into the core of the Earth?

Frantically, I clambered up beside the others. My muscles quivered and my hands shook. I fought to control the terror battering at my restraint.

"Oh, Andy," whispered Grace. "What do we do now?"

I shook my head. "Let me think." I felt for the drop-off with my foot and traced along the edge, wondering if we might pass to one side or the other. My worse fears were confirmed when I discovered the drop-off extended the width of the cave.

"Only one choice," I replied, turning back to them. "You keep the torch here. I'm going to swim ahead, see what's up there."

Mrs. Barton whimpered.

I tried to calm her. "Easy, Mrs. Barton. Take it easy. We're all scared, but we're going to make it out of here. Just don't go to pieces on me. . . ."

She looked at me, her lips quivering, her eyes brimming with tears.

"Or else," I added in mock severity, "I'll do what I said back on the mountain. I'll put you across my lap and spank you. Right here in the water."

She blinked in surprise. The children giggled. Grace snickered. I winked at the frightened woman. She tried unsuccessfully to smile, but she managed to reply, "I . . . I don't think that will be necessary, Mr. Stonecipher. Not this time."

I grinned. "Good." I handed her the torch. "Now, hold on to this until I get back." I looked at all of them. "I'm not going far, so don't worry. I'll be back."

Slowly, I eased into the water, the idea of the whirlpool in the back of my mind. I swam slowly by the glow of the torch into the darkness, using the breaststroke I learned as a youth with the Apache, trying to keep a hand in front just in case I swam into a wall.

Behind, the torch grew smaller. Suddenly, I touched a wall.

Pulling up to tread water, I discovered the cave took a turn to the right. The darkness was so complete that I might as well have closed my eyes. I continued swimming. Suddenly, I blinked.

Was that light ahead?

My hopes soared. I swam harder, and the light grew brighter. Moments later, my feet touched ground. I sloshed forward, seeing another bend ahead. When I reached that bend, I stopped, and grinned.

Ahead, the cave opened into a small pond, and beyond the pond sprawled a large valley. We'd made it.

I turned back for the others.

Thirty minutes later, we waded from the dark tunnel into the icy pond, lashed together with rags so none would stray during the swim through the darkness.

"Where are we?" Grace looked around the valley.

The sun was directly overhead. We had walked all night and through the morning. Best I could guess, we were some ten, twelve miles from the first valley. "I've never been here, but we're still not safe, not as long as those Comancheros are back there."

I found us a spot among a copse of loblollies and put the boys to building a fish trap. I cleaned and dried my Colt, our only remaining weapon.

Later, the boys returned with ten fat trout covered with brown specks. I built a small, smokeless fire over which we spit the trout.

Without warning, Mrs. Barton screamed.

I grabbed my Colt and spun, cocking the hammer in the same motion. Immediately, I relaxed.

My Apache brother stood facing us. Broad-shouldered, with a face fierce as a red-tailed hawk, he presented a frightening picture. "It's all right," I told her. "This is White Eye, my brother."

"You still move like the serpent," I said, turning back to him.

He grinned. "Your ears are the same . . . they hear nothing."

We looked at each other a moment, our eyes expressing our feelings. I stepped forward and offered my hand. We locked wrists.

"There is trouble," White Eye announced.

"Yes."

"Comancheros. We see at valley. They seek the gold." He stared at me accusingly.

"The gold is my fault." From the corner of my eye, I saw Otsie ease to his mother's side. "But once my friends were safe, I had planned to return to the valley. I remember the laws of our people."

My words satisfied White Eye.

"How did you find us?"

He nodded back to the north. "Smoke from valley. We watch as Comanchero search the cave. When they return with no one, I know that here we will find those for whom the Comanchero searched."

"Did you know it was me?"

"Not first, but later. I knew. You and me, we are the only ones Horse of Water told of the cave."

"Then he must be the one who placed the torches there."

"I do not know. I have never been inside the snake of darkness." He made an undulating gesture at the cave with his hand.

I nodded. "What about my friends here? Will you have them taken to Tucson?"

Grace exclaimed, "Andy!"

I waved her protests aside. "If you can get them safely to Tucson, I will return to the valley."

He shook his head. "You are not needed there. Our brothers have carried out the law of our people. You can return with your friends to Tucson. We have ponies."

"Then, the secret of the valley remains."

White Eye nodded.

"Good. I will take your offer of ponies. I will return them after my friends are safe." I gestured to the fire. "Come, eat."

He refused. "I return with the ponies soon."

An hour later, we rode out of the Baboquivari foothills and into the desert for Tucson. "We'll camp at Altar Wash tonight. We'll reach Tucson by mid-afternoon tomorrow."

Our spirits were high as we plodded through the sage and creosote. Not even the blistering sun could drain our excitement. Most of the afternoon was spent answering questions fired at me about White Eye and my years with the Apache.

Nor did the questions cease as we made camp in the arroyo that night. Between Otsie and John Edward, the others barely managed to slip in one or two questions. The boys prodded and poked at me about everything Apache from grub to gold, from fishing to fighting, from wickiups to wampum.

Finally, they tired. The day had been long, and within seconds after their heads touched their saddle blankets, they slept. Grace and I were the only two awake.

She smiled across the campfire.

"What now?"

I shrugged. For some reason, the prospective job in Oregon Territory was not as appealing now as it had been a few days before. "Something'll turn up. What about you?"

The firelight reflected off the wistful look on her face. "Back East, I suppose. Dev . . . that was my husband. Dev's parents offered us a place." She glanced at Otsie, who slumbered peacefully. "I don't know if I could raise a boy by myself out here." She looked around at the starry heavens. "The West is a mighty big place for a woman and small boy."

"Yeah." I nodded. "It's a big place for anyone."

I felt like I wanted to say more, like she wanted me to say more, but I didn't know what, so like the proverbial bump on a log, I remained silent.

After a few minutes, she nodded. "I guess I'll get some sleep now."

Lamely, I replied, "Yeah. We got a long ride tomorrow."

I lay back and stared at the stars above. We'd only been together a few days, but it seemed as if we'd known each other for years, as if the train wreck had happened far in the past. Tonight would be our last night together, and to my surprise, I felt a sense of regret.

Turning my head slightly, I peered at Grace's slender form on the saddle blanket. For several moments, I dreamed. "Who are you kidding?" I muttered to myself. "Who the Sam Hill are you kidding, you lockjawed broomtail buster?"

We rose early next morning and chewed on jerky while we saddled up. Just as I swung into the saddle, a guttural voice froze me to the marrow of my bones.

"That's far enough, cowboy."

Winchesters cocked, Tulsa Jack and the Papago stood on the rim of the arroyo. He sneered. "Your Apache friends got kinda lazy. They didn't look too hard." He motioned with the muzzle of his Winchester. "Get off them ponies, and you keep them hands away from that six-gun. Else that old woman is gonna have to find her a new head."

Mrs. Barton gasped. "You can't talk to me that way, you . . . Why, my husband—"

"Shut up and get down!" Jack bellowed.

We dismounted, and Jack, followed by the Indian, slid down into the arroyo.

Tulsa Jack nodded to the women and children. "Watch them, Injun. They cause any trouble, I'll skin your worthless hide. I got me a feller here to talk to."

The Papago's eyes met mine. He looked away quickly and motioned for the women and children to step back.

Jack strode up to me, gripping the Winchester by the forearm and the pistol grip. He stopped and planted his feet in front of me. "Yeah, I wanta talk to you, cowboy," he said, at the same time whipping the butt of the Winchester in an arc.

I jerked my head back, but the toe of the butt caught my chin a glancing blow, sending me spinning to the ground. Fireworks exploded before my eyes.

Dazed, I blinked against the pain, trying to focus my eyes. My head spun. Slowly, the sand inches from my eyes took shape.

"Get up, cowpoke. I ain't finished with you. Not

by a long shot. I'm going to hurt you bad.''

He kicked me on the side of my knee. I clenched my teeth. The pain cut through the fog in my brain.

I rolled over and lashed out with my feet.

Tulsa Jack laughed. ''Good try, but no prize.'' He stared down at me with a broad sneer slashing a thin scar across his bearded face.

I staggered to my feet. My head spun. I stumbled forward, sprawling to the sand.

His cruel laughter grew louder.

For several seconds, I lay motionless, trying to shake the dizziness from my brain. Behind me came the crush of boots in sand. When the footsteps halted, I threw myself in their direction, hoping to hit something.

I struck Tulsa Jack just below his knees, sending him backward. He cursed and sprawled on the sand. ''Why, you—''

Rolling to my feet, I grabbed for my six-gun, but the holster was empty. Frantically, I looked around, searching for the Colt. I spotted it, half-buried, behind Tulsa Jack.

''I'm going to blow your head off!'' he shouted, struggling to his feet.

The only choice I had was to beat him with my fists.

I leaped at him, grabbing for the Winchester before he could turn the muzzle on me.

He held tightly. We both struggled for the rifle, twisting and jerking, each attempting to break the other's grasp on the rifle.

Tulsa Jack spun, swinging me in an arc, but I clutched the Winchester with all my strength. He yanked on it, jerking me forward. I jerked back, yanking *him* forward.

Suddenly, he lunged, his momentum slamming him into me, sending us both to the sand. Gripping the Winchester desperately, we hit and rolled over and over, the butt and then the muzzle of the rifle sinking deep into the sand.

The muscular Comanchero rolled on top of me and tried to jam the Winchester against my throat. I shoved back. For several seconds, our struggle became a contest of strength. I weakened quickly. Just before he smashed the rifle into my throat, I shoved with my right arm and rolled to the left, throwing Tulsa Jack off balance.

He gave a startled shout when he fell aside, but the impetus of his falling yanked the Winchester from my hands. I jumped to my feet and started to leap at him, but Tulsa Jack was faster.

"Hold it!" he shouted, rolling into a sitting position and jerking the Winchester into his shoulder, centering the muzzle in the middle of my chest.

I hesitated.

His face twisted into a mask of rage. "I shoulda

killed you the first time I laid eyes on you." He tightened his finger on the trigger.

Behind me, Grace screamed. "Andy!"

Ten feet to my left lay the Colt. I lunged as the Winchester fired. Mixed in the cacophony of the explosion was a scream. I grabbed the Colt and rolled frantically, hoping to throw Jack's aim off.

I thumbed the hammer back and spun on my belly to face him, arm extended. My finger tightened on the trigger.

And I froze.

Tulsa Jack was sprawled on his back. At his side, the Winchester lay in the sand, its barrel split.

Hurriedly, I clambered to my feet, keeping the Colt aimed at the Papago while I checked on Tulsa Jack.

Jack was dead. The exploding barrel had sent a sliver of steel through his forehead. I glanced down at the Winchester. The barrel was full of damp sand, jammed deep when we rolled over in our battle for the rifle.

I looked back at the Papago.

He glanced at the inert body of his leader. A crooked grin curled his thin lips, and he lowered his Winchester. Our eyes met. He shrugged and turned back to the Mexican border.

I didn't stop him. Somehow, I had the feeling he was glad the entire incident was over.

After a dozen steps, he turned and looked at me. "I know nothing of your valley."

I studied him a moment, then holstered my Colt.

He gave me a cryptic smile and nodded.

I returned the gesture, and he walked away, his back straight, his eyes forward.

"Andy!"

Grace ran to me and threw her arms around my neck. "I was so scared," she said, her voice trembling.

Thick-skulled, I stood like a fencepost for several seconds before I realized she wanted my arm around her. Gently, I slipped my arm around her waist. To my surprise, I liked the feeling. For the moment, I was tongue-tied, and then I found my voice.

"What about the East? You still plan to go back?"

She looked up at me, her dark eyes twinkling. "Do . . . do you want me to?"

I was tongue-tied again, but I did manage to shake my head.

She smiled. "What does that mean?"

I hugged her to me again. "That means, no. I don't want you to go back East. I want you to stay."